BOOKS BY TIM MCBAIN & L.T. VARGUS

Casting Shadows Everywhere
The Awake in the Dark series
The Scattered and the Dead series
The Clowns
The Violet Darger series

RED ON THE

INSIDE

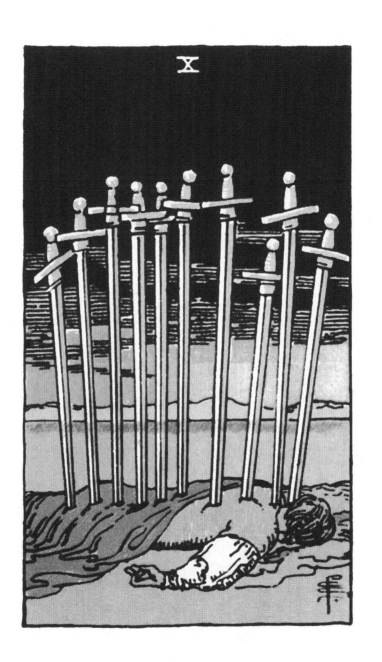

RED ON THE

INSIDE

CHAPTER 1

Houses sway around me on the sides of the street. I'm pretty sure I'm on the way back to Glenn's, but it's hard to tell. All of the houses out here look about the same, and the street signs are a little blurry at the moment. They should really consider color coding these things for the sake of excessively drunk pedestrians. I mean, it's hard enough to navigate with the lawns undulating on either side of me like this. Reading is out of the question.

So I might be lost, but I know this much: I'm moving away from the church, away from Farber and his minions with the tops of their heads shaved bald, away from the crowd rendered breathless in the presence of resurrection.

I walk. All of the booze makes the world want to spin around me, but if I keep walking in a straight line, it's more like the world tilts than spins. So, like I said, I walk.

I lean into it.

My head feels heavy, like there's a bowling ball sitting on my neck that wants to veer whatever direction the world is sloping at the moment. I have to concentrate to keep on the trajectory I want. It's sort of like steering a ship in an angry sea. It's OK, though, because I've done it all before. Once you get the hang of it, you never forget how to walk into a spin.

I realize that this whiskey has continued to make me

drunker and drunker, even though I stopped drinking some time ago. It's been so long since I drank liquor that I forgot how it worked a little bit. You chug and then wait. It's like it's on a time release.

To me, alcohol is like going underwater in a way. You're putting something dense between you and the rest of the world, some fluid that insulates you from everything else. It's like you get so isolated from everyone, you don't have to be scared or worry anymore, though. Nothing can touch you.

I guess I shouldn't be thinking about that so much. I should be pondering the intricacies of my possible resurrection after being burned alive. I mean, that's a pretty big deal, right? Getting torched at the bottom of a well? You don't run into that scenario every day.

I don't know. It either happened or it didn't. I'm too drunk for all of that critical thinking just now.

I reach the corner of a busy intersection, cars buzzing past. I lock my eyes on the gleaming orange hand telling me not to walk. I wait for the white glow of the walking person to flip on below. Well, I guess I lock my eyes on it a little too hard because the next thing I know I'm seeing double. It somehow makes the world stop spinning, at least, so that's good.

And then I realize that I'm not seeing double at all. I'm seeing the other world blurred over the top of this one. I say "other world" instead of "white world" because it's not white this time. It's a full color version of that translucent overlay like when I talked to Glenn in the mirror at that Mexican restaurant.

The other world sharpens into focus, and rolling hills of green grass take shape in front of me along with a couple of trees with buds on the tips of the branches. For a split second, I can feel the wind from this place whip across my face. It hisses through the blades of grass, and then the sound abruptly cuts out. And the wind feeling is gone as well, but the branches still wag, and the grass still lies down and pops up. It's like watching a silent movie.

The orange hand fades to black, and the white walker lights up. I set out to cross the street and also wade through the grass. I am in two places at once, and I'm very, very drunk in both of them.

To my surprise, the grass tangles around my feet and ankles when I take a step, and I almost trip. I didn't anticipate being able to feel it, but here we are. It's dense enough to constrict my range of motion, so I lift my feet high to better trudge through it. I realize that I probably look absurd as I traverse the crosswalk, doing a weird, kicky leg march. I'm not embarrassed so much as I kind of wish I could see it from afar.

I walk down a sidewalk past a few vacant buildings in the real world and climb a grassy knoll in the other world. It's kind of confusing to be going up and flat at the same time. My legs can feel the hill, and I step accordingly, but somehow I'm also walking on flat concrete.

And then I think about where Amity might be. Maybe I'll climb this hill and she'll be on the other side, and she won't even run since I'm not dangling any meat in her face this time.

I reach the top and let my eyes scan the hills.

No Amity. Nothing but grass.

But at least I can see it. The white world closed itself off from me, yes, but it seems I can drink my way to a glimpse. It's better than nothing.

And then a fist clenches in my gut, and the whiskey catches all the way up in a flash. It's usually not so sudden that the sickness comes over me, but today? Very much so.

I lean forward and vomit, and the foamy brown sick sprays into both worlds somehow, which is actually pretty awesome. It spatters about the grass in the other world, and splats the lip of a storm drain in the real world. I'm almost glad to be ill just to see this.

I give it a thumbs up without thinking about it, and then I imagine what this looks like to the cars passing by. Some guy hunching over the gutter, all giddy, with his thumb in the air like he's rating movies with Ebert, except instead of giving his take on <u>A Few Good Men</u>, barf cascades from his mouth like a waterfall of beer and booze and saliva and stomach juice.

Good times.

CHAPTER 2

As I get closer to home, the layer of semi-transparent grass running along the sidewalk fades, and then the other world flickers out all together. Interesting. So there's not necessarily a huge window there, but it's something.

Arriving at Glenn's, I let myself in. I figure he's still zonked, so I ease the door shut behind me and slide my shoes off all quiet like. I move toward the couch, but a sizzling noise stops me mid-stride. Then the smell hits me.

Oh man, someone's making breakfast. I smell eggs and some kind of breakfast meat and possibly a touch of cayenne pepper.

I change directions, passing by the dining room where I note the two halves of the puzzle sphere resting on the table like a clam shell, and head for the kitchen.

"Hey Grobnagger," Glenn says, unfazed by my ninja-like approach. "Jesus, is that puke on your face?"

"What?" I say.

I wipe around my mouth with my sleeve and examine the smear of brown foam it leaves.

"Oh yeah," I say. "Definitely puke."

My glance shifts from my sleeve to Glenn in time to see him close his eyes all disgusted.

"You know, we have napkins here on the premises," he

says. "And if you use the bathroom later, you'll even find toilet paper within arm's reach. Not sure if you've been using your sleeve in there this whole time, but I find the toilet paper gets the job done."

I tilt my head.

"Well, it sounds crazy, but I'm willing to try anything once," I say.

Glenn shudders, his shoulders shimmying. I don't know if he's picturing the nugget of puke foam on my face again or contemplating the logistics of sleeve wiping in the bathroom.

He serves up two plates of breakfast, and I tell him about Farber's return while we eat. He looks mildly concerned, but he doesn't say much. Then I talk about the drunkenness and how it opens a door to the other world. I leave out the part about vomiting every which way since we are eating. I finish my story, and we dine on in silence.

"Well, what do you think?" I say after a while.

"I think I'm taking two days to myself, maybe three," he says. "That's what I think. You know what I'm going to do? I'm going to go to Outback. I'm going to order a bloomin' onion. I'm not going to worry about all of this for a couple of days. And then I'll get back to you about what I really think."

For a guy that crafts such delicious food, Glenn has the worst taste in restaurants. I'd think he'd be into fine dining or weird little ethnic places no one has heard of, but instead he's all about riblets from Applebee's and stuff like that.

I take a bite of omelet with a lot of cayenne involved. The spice catches my throat just right and makes my eyes water.

"It's been too long since I've had a bloomin' onion," he says.

His eyes look all far away like his brain is playing a bloomin' onion memory montage. My only memories of Outback involve a commercial with John Madden back when he was in about 50% of all commercials. I don't remember for sure, but I think he probably said "Boom!" in there somewhere.

"So here's my question," I say. "Did I die and resurrect or what? I mean, did that tree bring me back somehow?"

Glenn answers all sassy like I'm being an idiot:

"Well, yeah, the tree brought you back," he says. "That's what it does."

"How was I supposed to know that?" I say.

"Well, if you weren't always rushing into trouble like a kid sticking his face into the blades of a fan, I was about to tell you before you touched it," he says.

"Oh," I say.

"Let me take a step back, though," he says. "The tree brought you back here. I can't say whether or not you resurrected. I'd assume not, but who knows?"

"Can't get a straight answer around here," I say, half under my breath.

I think about the blindfold. Damn. That'd be the perfect evidence, but I didn't look for it. If it was burned up at the bottom of the well, the fire was real. If not, it wasn't. I can't imagine going back to try to verify it, though. I'm not in a huge rush to get back down into that well, believe it or not.

"So here's another question," I say. "You said someone captured you, and lopped off the end of your foot, right? Who was it?"

He sighs.

"It's not like physical people caught me necessarily," he

says. "It's like a force in the air there or something. Like when you got strung up in the alley, right? Who knows who did that?"

He waves a chunk of omelet on his fork while he talks, sort of like a maestro.

"It's like how people talk about mother nature sometimes as though it is a sentient being asserting its will. I can't actually say it's sentient, though. I don't know. Sometimes I think it is, but other times I think it's more like a reflection of my imagination or my energy or something."

He finally eats the bite of omelet and loads another as he goes on.

"Whatever it is, it speaks in symbols, like it's trying to teach us things, yeah? But it wants us to earn it, not just to give it to us. Like your thing with the cup."

I think about this.

"Is it, like, God?" I say.

"No," he says. "I don't know. Truth is, you could call it that, maybe, but I don't think of it that way. I think of it as like the big consciousness, like how Carl Jung talked about the collective unconscious. If you look at the way he described it, he always worded it carefully. You could interpret the term as just meaning that the stuff in our right brain, our subconscious, contains all of these inherited instincts and archetypal understandings of things that have been passed down through the species, but he left the idea open that the term could refer to some communication between us, some divine connection. To me, it's all of us together, connected, but none of us at the same time. It's the place we connect to when we're dreaming. It's like a collective memory bank."

He shovels in another egg bite, chews for a second.

"They did this experiment in England with crossword puzzles," he says. "They had subjects do the puzzles when they were brand new and no one else had done them, and then they had the people do crossword puzzles that were a few days old and people all over London had done them. When the subjects did the older puzzles, their results improved by five percent."

I guzzle down the last of my coffee and pour a refill.

"Or another phenomenon is that IQ test scores keep going up," he says. "There's no other indicator that intelligence is increasing rapidly, but as more people take the tests, the average score goes up. As more people experience something – in this case particular tests – future people attempting it seem to inexplicably have an easier time at it. Maybe they can tap into this shared memory slash dream place, right?"

His eyes drift up and trace along the seam where the wall and ceiling meet.

"That's just one interpretation of it, though. That's what my gut tells me," he says. "I'm not saying it's right on some absolute level, or even that the conscious part of me believes it all the time."

"Wait a minute," I say. "I watched you rip open a door in a concrete wall and walk through it, into blindingly white light, and you still don't believe all the way?"

He laughs.

"All I'm saying is that I don't understand it or know what the hell it means," he says. "I mean, yeah, I can do a couple of things, but I'm like a guy that can play a couple of songs really well on the piano. People that don't know how to play the piano are impressed, but I'm no Beethoven. Knowing how to

9

do that stuff doesn't mean I have any goddamn idea what it is, what it wants, why we're here or any of that. My guess is no better than anyone else's."

He takes our plates to the sink and rinses them.

"Anyhow, we're not supposed to be talking about this," he says. "We're supposed to be talking about ribs and chicken on the barbie."

Great. More Outback stuff, I guess.

"OK, wait," I say. "Let's at least talk about the symbols around the tree before we move on to Aussie-tizers."

Glenn closes his eyes and sighs.

"Fine," he says. "I think the fact that you touched the side of the tree nearest the ocean is significant, so let's talk about that. The top of the ocean lurches in the form of sunlit waves. That's the water we typically know – for swimming, fishing and traveling over. Underneath, though, lies the darkness, the depths that would freeze us to death or crush us with inconceivable water pressure, the place where nightmares come alive in the form of creatures too weird to live in the light.

"In a way it represents the conscious and subconscious mind. The sun shines on the surface, but we know that there's so much more below we can't see. It can also be the depth of human emotions, the things down in your psyche that drive you to behaviors that you don't quite understand. But in a broader way it merely represents mysteries, deep and dark."

He sips his coffee.

"Sounds familiar, though, doesn't it?" he says. "Obsessing about the dark places."

"I guess so," I say.

"You're married to the sea, Grobnagger," he says. "In the

old days, the sailors that went out exploring didn't learn how to swim. They said that if they fell in or if their ship went down, their body should belong to the waves. There was a superstitious element, of course. Learning to swim was considered tempting fate."

"I'm not married to the sea," I say.

CHAPTER 3

Once we wrap up our symbol talk, things seem to simmer down into something more normal. We watch some cooking show where a guy makes a cabbage, sour cream, and bacon dish with the cabbage cut into strips to serve a pasta like role. Intriguing. Glenn writes down the recipe. He has a special notebook for writing down recipes like this. Unreal.

I nap my drunk off, sleeping into the afternoon, and Glenn wakes me in the evening for the much anticipated trip to the Outback. We head out to the car.

For once, the prospect of going to a restaurant doesn't bother me so much. Not that I'm looking forward to it, it's more that I don't care. I don't know if some kind of depression is settling over me or what, but I feel like the world burns dim about me, just the faintest glow like an oil lantern turned all the way down. After all of the excitement the past few weeks, it's not unpleasant, at least not in a painful way.

I feel nothing. Or close to that, anyway.

As we park, it occurs to me that I didn't even get nervous on the ride there. It barely even seems like it really happened. It feels like we got into the Explorer and transported to a primo parking spot by the front door.

Anyway, this is it, the Outback Steakhouse. As Glenn pulls open the door, the red glow of the neon light shines on his neck and lights up his beard from below. Something about the way the scarlet glimmer illuminates him makes me really look at him for the first time in a while. No navy blue cap tonight. His hair has grown out so I can see the border line where his blond highlights give way to all dark roots. I never knew he was dying his hair. I guess he wore the hat so much, I didn't get a great look. To trump this, he wears a pair of Elvis style sunglasses on the back of his head. Chrome. So I may as well be going out to eat with Guy Fieri. While I observe all of this, a hostess with bleached teeth and too much lip gloss asks us how many and tells us to follow her.

The chain restaurant sounds drone all around. Forks scrape plates. Dishes clink and chime against each other in the bus boy's tray. Ice cubes grind out wet sounds as they swirl in seas of cola. The small talk bleeds together into one wavering tone. All of the quiet nothings add up into a louder nothing, a static in the air, a buzz that leads nowhere.

I scan the room, but I find few signs of intelligent life.

I kid.

The people slurp and chomp and gnaw and smile. They all look the same. Up at the bar, they chug and take slugs and a fat lady has big jugs.

Sorry. Every once in a while I can't stop rhyming for some reason.

Sometimes I realize that I've been watching too much TV when I look around at the people in a restaurant or some other public venue and am astounded by how ugly they are. Now, ugly may be a strong word for what I mean here, but it fits in a way. They're just normal, but after so long looking at warped versions of humanity through the filter of the photogenic people cast for reality shows, things start to get weird. Even the people on TV that aren't very good looking often have striking features. I remember watching an episode of the Bachelorette once, where this guy with all close together eyes and a too huge smile had the Bachelorette girl visiting his family, right? And it astounded me how normal the family looked. The guy wasn't really handsome at all, but he looked like a TV person somehow. He had a remarkable face that sort of reminded me of a weird bird. By comparison, his family looked hollow and plain. Not especially ugly, but somehow not fit for TV. Not worthy.

And the girls on these shows are even stranger – primped to the point of creepiness, caked in makeup, surgically altered faces. They look all phony and inhuman with personalities to match more often than not, but then you see them around their families who look totally mundane, and it's like normal people are so much less stimulating that the level of plain seems dull. Dreary. Ugly.

Looking around the Outback, I see a lot of this. People buzzing around, standing, smiling, lost in conversations and thoughts and realities that I'll never know. Bodies that pull clothing taut in the wrong places. Faces you forget before you even look away. Not one of them looks worthy of the Bachelorette or the Amazing Race. They're hideously plain. And I know I'm one of them.

The waitress comes and goes in fast forward, bearing menus, then drinks, then food. I get a steak covered in a weird spice rub that I guess makes it more Australian. Not that great, but I bet John Madden would love every morsel of it.

The meal progresses quite rapidly. I almost feel like a sloth moving in slow motion while the world rushes around me at a pace I can't comprehend. And it occurs to me that the world isn't burning dimmer around me. I'm the one burning dimmer.

My mind drifts as we finish up our food, circling back to Louise over and over, which feels about like an ice pick to the heart. With my senses dulled and slowed, however, even a heart stab feels less painful than it should. I guess I'm thankful for that, but I don't know.

I feel like part of me should be angry, resentful. Part of me should harbor that little bit of hate that tells me I'm better off without her. I'll find someone better and so on. But even that part feels no hatred, no aggression. It just wants to crawl out into the cold sea and let the tide pull me away.

But it's fine. It's fine.

"Wouldn't it be great if life were this simple?" Glenn says, tearing off a deep fried onion chunk and dipping it in that weird orange goo. "If we could just find the things we enjoy and partake in them with no worries about the future or meaning or any of that?"

I think about it.

"Would it?" I say.

I must convey my snark a little too openly as he just glares at me. I guess I'm supposed to pretend that life would be great if we could just eat at Outback for eternity, like John Madden's vision of heaven.

"Do you ever stop and enjoy anything the world has to offer?" he says. "Or are you too busy living up in your head to appreciate what's going on around you?"

This from a guy with frosted tips and sunglasses on the back of his head.

I look around the restaurant. All the people swarm and flit about and churn their jaws endlessly like grasshoppers. I don't see why they bother. I don't see what drives them to it or what they get out of it. I could understand it, maybe, if I felt the people were seeing their own lives clearly, if they were seeing their own dreams clearly. But I don't think they are. I think they rush into marriages and families and careers that seem like what they want, but they have little interest in them once they're real. They're more interested in chasing some comfort at a restaurant, checking their phone every two seconds, hoping for something novel to happen. From moment to moment, they spend their lives seeking stimulation and little else.

Doesn't there have to be some illusion dangling in the distance for any of this to make sense? They prop up this dream of love and happiness. They gaze on it from afar as some goal they're vaguely pointed toward, but they don't really spend the days connecting with the people they care about on a genuine level. They spend the days concerned with comfort, with stimulation. They grind away their time working some job they care little about so long as that empty dream sits on the horizon in front of them.

And realizing that this is how the world operates around me makes most every encounter hollow. It renders most every experience impossible to enjoy. How can I connect to people who are perpetually distracted on purpose?

"Everything is all around you," Glenn says.

But it all means nothing to me.

CHAPTER 4

With his belly full of faux Australian cuisine, Glenn prepares to retire for the evening a little early. He steps into the hallway while brushing his teeth, and I get another quick glance at his stumped foot. The texture of the scar makes me shudder. The flesh puckers like maybe it was cauterized. I guess we got sidetracked before he could explain what the hell happened there. He said it was like an energy that captured him, right? Like a wave in the air. In my experience, air rarely exerts the force necessary to lop a foot off, but who knows?

Once he's down for the count, I'm left to my own devices. I flip through channel after channel, but nothing catches my interest.

I turn the TV off and sit, and the world gets so still. Nothing moves.

I know it's her before the headlights even twirl into the driveway. I walk out to the Lincoln, climb into the backseat. She's wearing a pirate blouse with puffy sleeves and a collar that winds up around her neck. She smiles when she sees me, but something about it looks timid.

"How have you been?" she says.

"Not bad," I say. "I don't know. Everything feels a little funny since, you know, I got set on fire and all of that. What's your take on that, by the way?"

"My take?" she says, eyelashes fluttering.

"Yeah," I say. "Do you think I resurrected or what?"

"Well…" she says. "After all that's transpired, I take it at face value, so yes. I think Randy burned you and you came back. And I think Farber set it all up. We all thought you were just going through rituals at an accelerated rate because of your dreams, but Farber wanted this for some reason. That's my take."

Oh yeah, I sort of forgot about that in a way. The guy that came back from the dead and probably wants to kill me. Just sort of slipped my mind. I suppose it would make sense for him to have a hand in these events. Interesting, though. I didn't expect her to buy in all the way.

"So Farber wants me to be, like, divine?" I say. "How does that help him?"

"It's hard to say," she says.

She chews her lip as both of us get lost in thought for a moment.

"Oh," I say. "I never asked how you've been, though."

She smiles, and I think I see a little tension drain from her shoulders.

"A little stressed," she says. "This Farber thing is hard to get a read on, but thankfully, the news isn't all bad."

I picture Farber standing at the lectern in the church, coughs racking his torso, purple veins bulging around his eyes.

"He seemed pretty sick," I say.

"Yes, he's quite weak. He's mostly slept since his… return," she says. "So the bad news is that he has formally declared you a false idol."

Now, I never really considered myself any kind of idol in

the first place, but what the hell? Pretty sure we both came back from the dead, jerk-off. Or maybe we didn't. I don't know.

"The good news?" she says. "He said he wants no harm to come to you. He said we're best to turn the other cheek and ignore the lost souls that know no better than to attempt to deceive us. He said, with great emphasis, we should leave you be."

"You know what? I can respect that," I say.

"Still," she says. "I could never trust him after what happened before. If it means you're OK for now, so be it, but I'm concerned."

"I'm not that worried, really," I say. "What's Farber going to do? Cough on me?"

She grimaces.

"That would be pretty gross," she says.

"Plus, I figure you've got those guys out in the car watching me at all times, right?" I say. "Those guys have large firearms on their persons, correct?"

"They're armed," she says.

"See? If Farber comes at me, we'll get to see a new magic trick," I say. "One of your men will hover a bullet into his skull with a simple squeeze of the trigger."

The silence hangs in the air moment, the conversation pausing on that awkward note.

"You seem a little down lately," she says.

"Yeah, I don't know," I say. "I've been tired."

I remember the numb that came over me at the Outback, but what's the use in describing it?

"That's all it is?" she says.

"Yeah," I say.

19

I smile. She looks like she doesn't quite buy it, but she doesn't say anything. I can live with that. It's not worth explaining these things anymore. Words are wind. They fly out into the air and float away into nothing.

"So what's up with the League these days?" I say. "Everyone has real weird haircuts now, eh?"

"I'm afraid I'm out of the loop some as of today," she says. "The haircut people won't talk to me. I thought about taking an electric razor to my head, but it wouldn't help. Everyone knows I'm your friend."

I pick at the door handle with my fingernails.

"Yeah, you're getting blackballed. You finally know what it's like to be a Grobnagger," I say. "Do you think it's unsafe for you to keep hanging around there?"

She rolls her eyes.

"Oh, I'll be fine," she says.

"I never really thought about it," I say. "But this all kind of means the Sons of Man took over, right? They used Farber's resurrection story to charm everyone, and now the whole league is along for the ride."

"It would seem so," she says.

She looks far away.

I lie on the couch in the dark, drifting to that half asleep state almost immediately. I feel empty inside, like one of those crispy locust husks stuck to the side of a tree, all hollow and shit.

The sheet goes from cool to warm to hot against my skin, and the blanket grips me in a way that almost feels like a hug. It's a knit blanket. I'm not sure what the material is, but it has some weight to it.

Red on the Inside

As sleep takes me, I think maybe this is the best life actually gets. Warm and secure and floating away from reality.

CHAPTER 5

When the morning comes, the light glares in and disturbs the peace. It's not even glints of sunlight that might provide some biologically wired reward. This light is gray and cold. Do not pass go. Do not collect the burst of endorphins.

From what I can tell, no part of me wants to get up. My joints are all stiff. My muscles ache. My mind only wants to lie in the dark forever where the light will never wake me.

But I get up anyway.

I look out the window. Dead leaves litter the front lawn, the world muted to shades of brown and yellow. It's weird how fall sneaks up and chokes the green out of everything all sly like. And for a split second the grass field from the other world flashes in my memory. Still green over there, I suppose.

"Mornin' Grobs," Glenn says as I step across the threshold to stand in the kitchen doorway.

Talking seems like too much effort, so I nod a return greeting. He holds court in his kitchen just like the good old days, oven-mitted hands pawing at a tray of baked goods, setting it on the counter. At first I think he's made a homemade version of those pecan pinwheel things, but no. Cinnamon rolls.

He pipes frosting out of a legit pastry bag. Or maybe it's icing. I don't know the difference.

Red on the Inside

I sit at the snack bar, and we eat.

We don't talk much, and the things that we do say aren't all that interesting.

I chug coffee between bites, and it wakes me up, but not all the way somehow. It's like my eyes are wide open, and I feel all the physical feelings of being alert, but my brain is still a little bit dead.

It's enough that I have a hard time staying tuned into this disjointed conversation we're having that is punctuated with long pauses, loud chewing, and coffee slurps, but this is the second day of Glenn's culinary walkabout, so we make plans to go to Chili's.

Wait.

You know what? He makes plans to go to Chili's. I have no say in these matters. I am just along for the ride.

The cinnamon rolls are pretty good, though.

After a morning spent watching awful daytime TV, we sit around in silence much of the afternoon. I read part of the introduction to a Kierkegaard book, but even the translator's intro is a little hard to follow. Probably doesn't bode well for ol' Grobnags' chances of digesting the actual text, but whatever.

Glenn reads some book about war. For real. I can almost remember the title, but wait, that's right. I died of boredom before I could finish reading the cover.

On the plus side, he does not bust into the baby back ribs jingle at any point during our reading session. This is a major victory for good taste and decency, though I admit that a certain part of me is a little disappointed. I could have chimed in with that baritone "barbecue sauce" at just the right moment, and now I may never get that opportunity.

A few times while reading the mind numbing words of Kierkegaard's translator, I get the urge to ask Glenn more questions to clarify whatever happened to him in the other world, but... Well, I know he doesn't want to talk about any of it for at least another day, but I kind of don't care anyway. Even when I think of the questions, it feels more like I'm pretending to care.

Makes no sense, right? Right.

I mean, a lot of shit hangs in the balance: My life. Amity's life. Other stuff, I think.

So I should care, but it all seems like too much of a hassle just now. And I have this feeling that it won't lead to anything anyway. Not really.

I read some more. Now Kierkegaard has his own introduction to the writing. I don't know. Getting pretty frustrated with the endless introductions. Without thinking, I speak:

"You think Farber wants to kill both of us?" I say.

Glenn looks up from the war book and just stares at me through the glasses perched on the tip of his nose while this question processes... or doesn't.

"What?" he says.

"Do you think Farber wants to kill both of us? Or just me?"

He turns back to the book.

"I don't concern myself greatly with what Riston Farber wants," he says.

"He must have been the one that wanted Randy to set me on fire, though, right?"

"It seems likely."

"Did he want me dead, though, or did he want me to resurrect?"

"Look, I told you I'm not getting into this today, but I'll set something straight for you right now. Riston Farber is a phony. He's a con-man. I'm not worried about him or anything he might have planned."

Sheesh. Bite my head off.

The pieces don't fit together in a way that makes sense, though. If they just wanted to kill me, why go about it in a way that semi-fit the resurrection rituals Randy alluded to? But why would they want me to come back from the dead? Was it just a test? That wouldn't make much sense either considering Farber had seemingly been burned up some weeks before.

As these thoughts circle toward the drain in my head, Glenn squints my way and gives me the nod. You know, the, "We're going to Chili's now," nod.

I stand and stretch. It occurs to me that I don't even get that twinge of nervousness that I usually get just before an excursion such as this anymore. But am I growing used to all of this additional stimulus, or am I giving up?

At least I'm not to the point of wearing sweat pants in public yet. There's still hope.

We file out to the damn Explorer, which Glenn starts with a thunderous muffler free rumble. I lean back in my seat, and the leather is just cold enough to chill my skin through my t-shirt and give me goose bumps. I don't mind, though, somehow.

I close my eyes and drift right down to the almost sleep state again. The volume of the exhaust gets turned down until it sounds really far away. I guess I'm still awake but just barely.

It's weird to go down so quickly. It's like my anxiety is

turned off. I don't feel like myself much. I don't like it in some ways, but it does numb everything out. Maybe that's why I don't mind the cold. It fits the numb.

Time goes faster somehow, and then we're parked at Chili's, and then we're shuffling inside, and it all feels like something I'm observing, like it's not quite real.

I don't feel it at all.

And we're seated. And there are drinks and mozzarella sticks.

Glenn orders the baby back ribs. Duh.

I don't know what to get. I'm not even hungry, really. I wind up going for chicken fingers. I almost feel like I should apologize for this choice, but I don't know. It seems like they'd be easy to eat. Slather those things in some kind of sauce so they slide right down, I figure.

I put my head down while we wait for the food.

"You all right?" Glenn says.

"Tired," I say.

If I let myself, I could fall asleep right here with my forehead adhered to the table. Don't I know I should be readying steak knives or finding a swordfish or something to plunge into a potential attacker's throat? Especially now that I've been set on fire and zombie Farber came back from the dead to say bad things about me.

Whatever, though.

I let myself drift, and the black grows blacker, and the Chili's sounds fade out into nothing.

I float in empty space. It is warmer than the real world, and I can let go all the way. Maybe that's all I've really wanted all along.

"Dude," Glenn says. "Food's coming."

The black dissolves to light. I sit up and hear myself slurp saliva from the corner of my mouth. The waitress smiles at me and sets my plate of chicken fingers onto the little puddle of drool in front of me. I think I forgot to smile back. I hate when I realize that too late.

I dunk the chicken into sauce the color of the Dalai Lama's robe. It doesn't taste like much, but I chew and swallow all the same.

Glenn's eyes take on a demonic look as he regards the meat in front of him, and his lips look all juicy. This kind of freaks me out. He mutters to himself as he tears into the ribs, gnawing hunks of meat and gristle from the bones.

"Oh yeah, babe," he says just above his breath.

Barbecue sauce smears about the perimeter of his maw like maroon lipstick applied on a roller coaster. His mustache looks like a loaded paintbrush. I think about telling him about this, but hey:

His mustache. His problem.

Still, I have no choice but to stop and watch him eat for a while. It's a ferocious act. It's like watching a lion rip apart a gazelle on the Discovery Channel.

"Pretty good, huh?" I say.

His eyes do not leave his plate.

"Off the chain," he says. "Big time."

Glenn watches Top Chef in the evening, but I can't stay focused. I keep involuntarily leaning over onto the arm of the couch and then snapping back upright to try to pay attention.

A chef wearing a cabbie hat is making sea bass tacos, if I'm understanding this correctly – a ballsy move in my opinion. I think he is overcooking the sea bass, but then the tiredness hits again, and I'm staring at the floor, tipping until my shoulder meets the arm of the couch, and then – BAM – my eyes are closed.

This is getting weird. I'm all slowed down, and I can't keep up with something as mindless as a TV cooking competition. I was kind of wondering how those sea bass tacos would come out, too.

Once again I hover in that place just short of unconsciousness. My body grows warm where it touches the couch, though the tip of my nose is freezing. My thoughts get clear and calm.

And I realize that depression – like the kind I'm feeling now – is the only peace I've found in this life. When my serotonin levels decrease, and the light inside dims to the faintest glow, I can finally keep my thoughts still for a while. The sad takes me to a tranquil place. It shuts off the endless levels of self consciousness, that bottomless well of inwardness that keeps me awake in the dark.

Maybe it's better to not fight it. Maybe it's better to stay down.

Because I feel cold inside and useless and worthless, but it's also a form of peace. And when it's like this, I know it will be okay in a way. Even if I float face down to the end, and there's no one to help me.

It will be a relief.

CHAPTER 6

I dream of the woods.

Green surrounds me so thick that I can't see more than a few feet in any direction. I bend branches out of the way and step forward. Somehow I already know it's a dream, so I kind of think it doesn't matter which way I go.

Maybe.

The trees get thicker, and the green thins out a bit, at least on the ground. The leaves above form a canopy that blocks out the light, so I walk in the endless shade. I realize that these things mean I'm getting deeper into the forest.

Even with the growth on the ground a little less full than it was a moment ago, I still can't see much. There's enough brush to block my vision, even if I can pick my way through a little easier than before.

Leaves hiss as they brush against my shorts.

Wait.

Shorts?

I look down at my legs.

OK, I'm wearing cargo shorts. No idea.

And as I gaze upon khaki shorts that I don't recognize at all, it occurs to me that I have this nagging feeling buried somewhere in my thoughts, a feeling like I've forgotten something important. The sensation has fluttered there beneath the surface this whole time, though I just now drew it into the light. It almost feels like an itch.

I move through an area cluttered with a bunch of tiny trees about the girth of a pool cue, some of which have those red cone shaped clusters of something on them.

I feel lost, like I'm just meandering. I mean, I'm trying to walk in one direction, but the undergrowth seems to push me where it wants me to go, which might be in circles. I'm not sure.

Can you be lost if you have no destination? Or are you always lost in that case? I can't decide.

Branches and leafy bits reach out for me and try to prod at me as I walk, so I slap them away. Look, I'm usually not so violent with plant life, but what the hell? Leave me alone.

Wait.

I stop.

I listen.

Did I just hear…

The wind picks up, and the leaves above rustle against each other. It's a scrape and swish that sounds like when you first put the needle on a record. Anyway, there are no other sounds.

Maybe it was nothing, the wind and shit.

I walk on, kicking through stems and stalks and seed pods and other plant body parts.

The light seems to dim a little more around me, and I stop again. The hair on the back of my neck stands up. A tickle crawls across my skin like fingertips creeping over all of me. I don't know why.

And then that forgetful feeling perks up again, but I realize that it's not exactly forgetful after all. It's more like I'm missing something. Something is happening in these woods, or maybe something is being transmitted to me from elsewhere, and I'm missing it. It's like there's a wave in the air intended for me, but I can't quite tune the radio right. It can only muster an unpleasant sensation in my frontal lobe.

I bring my hands to my forehead. My head hurts, and something about all of this makes me feel physically nauseous. My stomach tightens up like it wants to blow, and I get these queasy little muscle shimmies in my obliques, so I guess they want to chip in and do their part in the heaving process. The combination is overwhelming.

But instead of a vomity spray, laughter spews forth from my lips.

Now, none of this is funny, of course. Just the opposite, really. Feeling lost and sick in a darkening forest with an overwhelming sense that I'm missing something of vital importance? It's all so serious that it feels inappropriate to laugh.

Well, I guess the cargo shorts are a little funny, at least.

Anyway, I feel like a crazy person, hunched over in the middle of the woods, laughing like a fool. I can see the rounded tops of my cheeks tinted the hue of pink lemonade at the bottom of my field of vision. My eyes are opened too wide, and they have this sting to them like I can almost feel an electric current flowing through there. The laughter keeps spilling out of me oblivious to all of these unpleasant feelings, and the dread in my gut just grows and grows.

See, I want to stop laughing, but I can't. Any notion of self control careens away from me with the rest of my thoughts, jumbling themselves up into blasts of word salad that fire every time I try to collect my wits.

Am I hallucinating?

Wait.

I stop laughing.

I definitely heard something this time.

A voice.

I wonder if this is what it's like when you start hearing voices?

I suck in a breath all loud like a baby that finally stopped crying, and I can hear my heartbeat thrumming in my ears.

I realize that I'm in a karate stance, which is weird because I don't know any martial arts stuff at all. I guess I watched The Karate Kid, Part II a lot at the babysitter's house when I was a kid. I might have picked up some shit.

Trying to think of any signature moves in there that I could unleash if necessary... I remember there were definitely bonsai trees which seemed pretty temperamental. You had to take care of them just right or Mr. Miyagi would go apeshit. I guess I don't know if that knowledge will be very helpful here.

The voice comes in more clearly, but I can only make out every fourth word or so. The rest sounds all smeared and watery like when you can sort of hear the TV while you sleep on the couch.

"apologize... making... like this... didn't... work... hear me?... Hello?"

It's a girl's voice. It doesn't sound familiar.

I ease out of my karate stance and squint my eyes. My brain starts tumbling all of the pieces of information around. I get that feeling like I got back in high school, when my brain would switch over to autopilot while I did 25 algebra problems in a row for homework. I think maybe I'm about to realize something.

The voice drones on, mostly sounding like Charlie Brown's teacher, and I swivel my head to look at the woods around me. It's all so green. Almost too green, like the saturation is turned up a little. It reminds me of the grass field I vomited in the other day.

Oh yeah. That's it. This isn't a normal dream. I'm there. I'm in the other world.

This raises more questions, of course… How did I get here? I've never come through via sleep. Only seizures, drunkenness, and whatever happened to me in the bottom of the well. (Death, I think, though I haven't ruled out drugs.)

Also, if this is the other world, then the voice is really happening. It's not just something I'm dreaming. So who it is becomes relevant. Plus, where the hell is it coming from?

It definitely sounds weirdly detached and distorted, almost like it's being broadcast over a PA. I try to decide if it's literally in the air around me or in my head. It's hard to say for sure, but I think the latter seems more right. So what the hell does that mean?

"there?… hear me?"

"I can hear you," I say. "Kind of."

There's a pause.

"… s'good… think…. work."

"I can't understand," I say. "Who are you?"

The voice gurgles 3 syllables of gibberish and stops.

"What?" I say.

"Amity."

It takes a long, slow motion moment to sink in. I rub my

eyes like that could help clear things up. I've seen her. I've read her words. In many ways I feel like I know her, but I've never heard her voice.

Until now, I guess.

"How?" I say.

"brought… here… concentrating… focusing."

She sounds stronger than I imagined, like a girl that wouldn't hesitate to get right in someone's face if she felt it necessary. Not bitchy, though. Just strong. When I was a kid, that was the kind of girlfriend I wanted. A fearless girl. A violent one.

"Where are you?" I say.

"Out… forest… you?"

"I'm in the woods, too," I say.

I try to think of a way I can find her. I run forward, doing swim moves with my arms to help me move between branches. Once I've made it a hundred feet or two, I stop and try to decide if the droning voice sounds any closer or farther, but I can't tell. I don't know if it'd make sense. It's like it's being broadcast somehow, so I don't think it'd get louder as I got closer, maybe.

Shit.

Here we are again. Another opportunity to figure some of this stuff out that's maddeningly close and still out of reach entirely.

"I don't know what to do," I say.

She babbles more words I can't understand. I realize that this isn't that much different than many of the conversations I have with people in a certain way. We can't actually communicate. I can transmit my ideas, but I get nothing back but meaningless noise. Or at least that's how it feels.

I sit down, and ferns reach over to tickle my calves. Stupid cargo shorts.

I don't know what to do. I wipe my fingers across my brow, and my hands feel all rough.

Shit.

Someone tell me what's going on. Someone tell me what to do.

Amity gibbers out more and more nothing. Or maybe it's something, but I can't understand it.

The sky blushes around me, going red like the sun is setting. As I remember that there's no sun out here that I've seen, the red glow washes out all of the green and overtakes me. I watch it all disappear.

CHAPTER 7

When I wake the next morning, my eyes still have that hallucinogenic sting, and I feel a similar, almost sizzling, sensation in my skull about three inches back from the center of my forehead. I sit up, and the ache of tiredness unfolds in the lines on my face and the curve in my upper back where my shoulders stoop. It doesn't feel like I got much rest.

Then again, the woods, the voice – it all feels so far away now. Argh. Is it possible it was just a dream? I guess. I mean, I guess it's possible.

Damn it. Constantly trying to decide what's real and what's not? Starting to get old. Sure, it's a barrel of laughs at first, but…

I stand and pull my shoulders back to stretch, and some tendon or cartilage or something seems to give just under my sternum. My torso quakes, and then there's sharp pain.

The words "ruptured it" pop into my head. Goddamn it! Hopefully I didn't actually rupture anything, but one of those little crab forks stabs me in the chest every time I take a breath now. So that's good.

I shuffle into the bathroom and make eye contact with my grimacing reflection for a split second before I rip open the medicine cabinet. (Note to self: Don't grimace. Ever. You look like Scut Farcus when you do it, and nobody thinks you're cool.

I'm sorry.)

I dig through Glenn's pill bottles. There are a lot, and let's be honest. Probably at least some of these pills have something to do with pissing constantly. From what I understand based on watching the commercials during Jeopardy, all old people turn into weird, leaky piss machines that need some combination of medication and/or diapers just to make it through the day. So there's something else to look forward to.

I finally find the ibuprofen, pop open the bottle, and wash a couple down with a handful of water from the sink. For some reason ibuprofen is the medicine that works for me. I know other people that like all that Aleve and shit, but not me. Ibuprofen gets rid of headaches and sore muscles and even heartburn pain for me. I think if a doctor told me I had ebola, I'd try two ibuprofen. Just in case.

I hunch as I walk out to the kitchen. It seems to hurt less if I keep my chest a little concave, though I probably look like Igor about to go off about Abby Normal's brain.

"Morning," Glenn says.

He sticks his lips out as he takes in my Quasimodo gait, and it looks like his mustache is reaching out to touch his nostrils.

"What's with the silly walk?"

"Well, I ruptured it," I say.

He wiggles his nose and lips and for a split second his mustache is in his nose. I imagine it feels like sticking a Brillo pad into your snout.

"What?" he says.

"I don't know," I say. "I stretched this morning and something popped in there or something."

I rotate my hand over the ruptured sternum area.

"Felt like a rubber band snapping or something."

For a second I picture my insides like the engine of a car: belts coiling around wheels, pistons pumping, spark plugs sparking.

Glenn seems distracted, though. He peels open a foil sleeve and puts some Pop Tarts into the toaster oven.

Wait. Pop Tarts? Aren't we supposed to have some gourmet breakfast? Something isn't right here.

When he goes to microwave two mugs of leftover coffee from last night, I put my foot down.

"What the hell?" I say, and then the crab fork pierces my heart pretty good, so I hunch more.

"What?" he says.

"Are you feeling OK?" I say.

He pauses with the microwave door open, the wedge of light from within illuminating the, "I heart fishing," coffee cup in his hand.

"Oh. Yeah, I don't know. Weird dream, I guess," he says.

A dream.

A weird dream.

And the world goes into slow motion. A crowd bolts upright into a standing ovation, the applause crashing everywhere. Fireworks burst in a night sky. All of the dogs for blocks yip and howl at each other like there's a full moon.

I want to throw back my head in ridiculous, Amadeus style laughter, but the crab fork would make me pay dearly, so I let out a single, "Ha!"

Glenn glares at me. I realize he was privy to neither the fireworks nor the ovation since they were imaginary. Fair enough.

"Let me guess," I say. "You dreamed of the woods."

He just looks at me, his mouth partially agape, and then the microwave beeps.

"Amity," he says. "Did you... Could you hear her?"

I nod.

"I couldn't make out most of what she was saying."

"Me neither."

The toaster oven ring-a-dings, and Glenn plops the Pop Tarts on a plate, which he holds toward me. I take one and bite it. Hard to tell if it's cherry or strawberry.

I never thought about how British the name Pop Tart sounds until just now. As a breakfast item, it's not too bad, but the edge parts are weirdly dry. It takes some conscious effort to power the crusty bits down my gullet so I can talk, and they scrape on the way down.

"So if it happened to both of us," I say, my voice a touch hoarse. "It was really her, right? She was really talking to us."

Glenn chews, swallows, thinks it over.

"I'd think so," he says.

He sets his Pop Tart on the plate and gets the coffee out of the microwave, placing one in front of himself and sliding the other my direction. I take a sip. It's pretty good for being a day old. I think it makes the Pop Tart seem better, too.

"Thinking back, she seemed to be asking if it worked at first," he says. "And asking if I was there."

"Yeah," I say. "That might be what she said to me, too."

He nibbles at the dry crust and washes it down with coffee.

"Makes me think she did it on purpose," he says. "I mean, that she somehow pulled us there."

"Could be," I say.

39

"She's been out there a long time. I guess she could have learned more than a few tricks by now."

"You spent some time with her, right?" I say. "What is she doing out there?"

"What do you mean?"

"I mean, why doesn't she go to the tree or something like that to get out of there?" I say. "She's been in the other world for like eight months or something in our time."

"Well, there could be a lot of reasons," Glenn says. "You've been there. It gets weird. You're not necessarily thinking clearly the whole time, and it's not intuitive to find your way around."

His eyes look all shifty for a second. He takes a slug of coffee before he finishes his thought.

"Anyway, I'm not sure that she wants to come back."

I run this sentence back and forth a few times in my head to try to make sense of it.

"You're not sure?" I say. "What does that mean?"

"Well, she said she doesn't want to come back. She told me that."

What the shit! Ever since the seizures started, nothing has made any sense. And yet I am somehow not surprised. Why shouldn't our mission be rooted in nonsense like every other goddamn thing?

I try to picture Amity wandering around, crossing deserts and trekking through woods. It's an odd choice to stay out there. In a way I can understand it, but…

"So all of this effort is to save someone that doesn't want to be saved?" I say.

Glenn curls his fingers into his mustache like he's thinking about trying to claw it off, but instead he releases his mustache

40

claw grip and slams the heel of his hand on the countertop.

"She can't just stay out there, Grobnagger," he says. "That's no life."

I think this over. I think maybe it's all no life – no matter what you do – at least if you think about it hard enough, but I don't tell Glenn this.

"I guess if she was trying to contact us, there's still a reason to find her," I say. "Even if she doesn't want to leave."

"Yeah," Glenn says. "Yeah, there you go. See? I knew you'd get it."

I eat the last of my Pop Tart and wash down the grainy bits with lukewarm coffee.

"So we're going to find a way to go back and get Amity, yeah?" I say. "Maybe now would be a good time for you to tell me what happened to you before. With your foot and everything."

He takes a deep breath.

"You're probably right," he says.

He rinses out his coffee cup, hesitates a moment as if deciding whether or not to refill it, and takes a seat at the snack bar.

CHAPTER 8

"When I try to remember it," he says, and then he stops himself to gather his thoughts. "You ever watch a movie you know you've seen before, but you somehow can't remember how it ends? You might remember a few key moments, but you can't quite pin down where it's going even though you've already seen the damn thing? And that somehow makes you more enthralled to keep watching to find out? Like it's almost more perplexing to have seen it and forgotten?"

"Yeah, I think so," I say.

"Well, thinking back on what happened there is kind of like that," he says. "I remember a lot of it, maybe most of it, I think, but I can't quite put the sequences together in an order that makes sense."

He stands, refills his mug and shoves it in the microwave.

"I can't stop thinking about it, trying to make it all fit together," he says. "You want more coffee?"

"Well, yeah," I say. I push the mug across the counter toward him.

"I remember finding Amity in a cornfield," he says.

"OK, so who do you think is planting corn over there?"

"How should I know?" he says. "Anyway, thinking about it now, I feel like I was trying to get away from something, but I'm not sure. I was running through this field, crashing through

42

row after row of corn, and I saw something out of the corner of my eye. I stopped dead on the spot and looked, and there she was, just sitting Indian style in the middle of a field."

I picture her sitting in the field, and in my imagination she is meditating.

"I just realized that sitting Indian style means like Hindu meditation type sitting," I say. "For some reason I always thought of Native American style 'Indians' before. Didn't really get it."

Glenn looks at me for a long time.

"First of all, you're racist," he says.

"What? How is that racist?" I say. "I'm not racist!"

He grunts, thinks it over.

"Fine. Whatever," he says. "I guess you're not necessarily racist."

He sips his coffee before he goes on:

"But you are like a regular Sherlock Holmes when you wield those powers of deduction like that."

"Sorry for not understanding the origin of an idiom that was probably imprinted into my vocabulary when I was three years old."

"Can I finish my story now, or are you going to defend your idiocy at some length?"

"Finish it."

"Perfect," he says, a puff of breath exiting his nostrils just after that reminds me of a pouting Boston Terrier. "Like I said, I found Amity. She was a little non-responsive at first, just staring off into space. I probably said seven or eight different sentences to her and tried to squat and hug her, but she didn't move. It wasn't until I pulled her wrists to help her stand up that she kind of came around."

"Do you think she really was meditating?" I say. "Like in a trance or something?"

"It's possible," he says, tilting his head. His eyes flick back and forth a few times. "She was definitely hiding things from me during our time together."

"What do you mean?"

"I don't know," he says. "More than once, I got the sense that she knew things. Her own version of my few parlor tricks, right? But she never wanted to talk about what all she had seen or done there. And she often wandered off on her own. I'd find her sitting by herself. And then later, after she told me she didn't want to leave, she wouldn't explain herself. She reverted to blank stare mode."

His index finger grinds at the corner of his mouth like there might be some Pop Tart stuck there.

"She didn't quite seem like herself, at least not all the way," he says. "But she was so peaceful that I didn't think much of it, you know?"

"How long were you together?" I say.

He buries his forehead in his palms.

"I have no idea. Time is fucked there, Grobnagger. You know that. There's no day and night there, so it becomes impossible to keep track of time. I mean, there are places where it's night, but..."

He trails off, and we sit in the quiet for a while.

"We walked a long way," he says. "Walked across a stretch of flat land for what must have been days, grass plains mostly. But eventually that gave way to a more arid climate. Still flat, but all dried-out red Earth with cracks etched everywhere into it, yeah? Looked like the surface of Mars or some goddamn thing."

"Where were you going?" I say.

"Hell if I know. Thing is, I felt like I was headed for something. I felt like a purpose drove my actions. I just don't know what that purpose was. I can't even say if I knew what it was at the time and don't remember or if I never knew. That make any sense?"

"Yeah," I say. "I guess I felt kind of like that when I was there."

"So the terrain got hillier and rockier with a few taller trees here and there. Pines or maybe firs, I guess. And then it got dark. Like I was saying earlier, there are places there where it's always night with the only light coming from the moon. The night seemed awesome in a way. Having gone so long without it, I really wanted to get a night's sleep out there. You don't really get tired there. I think you take breaks and sit down solely out of habit, you know? Out of a fondness for it, or the nostalgia factor of doing it or something like that."

"Yeah," I say.

"We didn't have much to set up a camp with, but we started a fire."

"You started a fire? Rub two sticks together or what?"

"Nah, Amity had a lighter."

"A lighter? Did she take that over there, or find it or something?"

"Don't know. You really get hung up on the minutiae, Grobnags."

"Sorry. I just don't understand it."

Glenn shrugs.

"Anyway, we slept by the fire, yeah? There were no stars in the sky, but the moon hung up there so huge. Not quite full, but it seemed close. It was a weird sleep, for me at least. It was like as soon as I closed my eyes I was dreaming crazy stuff. I was lost. My brain coughed out gibberish over and over, and all of the scenery about me kept morphing so I was repeatedly shifted into new locations. Like I was moving from set to set on some studio lot. So I was lost in the woods, then lost in the frozen tundra, then lost in the desert, then lost in the jungle. Just nonsense, you know? But aggressive nonsense, somehow. Like my mind was yelling it at me the whole time."

He scrapes his thumbnail on the handle of his mug, and it shrieks a little.

"When I woke up, Amity was gone. I really didn't think much of it at first. Like I told you, she'd wandered off before. I always found her sitting nearby, gazing out into the distance."

He turned to look out the window over the sink. I don't know if he was pantomiming Amity staring out into nothing or doing so himself.

"I kicked sand over where we set up the fire and called out for her a few times, started looking around for her. But she was gone. I knew almost as soon as I started looking that I wasn't going to find her."

"I thought you said you got trapped," I say. "No wait. 'Captured.' That's what you said."

"Will you let me finish?" he says.

"Yeah, sorry."

"I walked in the dark a while. I was in a valley with rock walls on either side of me, so I just followed the path dictated by the terrain. Soon I could hear the faint rumble of thunder, which seemed to be getting closer and closer as I advanced.

"Somehow I wasn't too upset about being separated from Amity. I mean, I missed her already, but out there it just feels like everything that happens makes sense. You feel like it's all for a reason. Or I do, anyway.

"The sky turned gray a little, like that half light before dawn. Now the thunder was really rumbling all over. I came around a bend, and I saw a tower on the cliff to my left. I could really only see the silhouette of it. Looked like a spire off of a castle or something but on its own.

"And just as I stopped walking to gaze up at it, lightning flashed. Everything lit up for a fragment of time, and the bolt of light split the sky and struck the tower. The thunder hit immediately and shook the Earth.

"The rumble rolled down the canyon, and the ground vibrated beneath my feet, and hunks of rock rattled and scraped against each other all around me. And as the flash of light died out, I saw fire in its place. Flames licked out from the roof, and it was like a delayed reaction, like watching a tree get chopped down when the top of the tower crumbled away a moment later.

"Blocks of stone separated from the wall and fell in all directions. The roof spire tilted out of place and slid off of the structure, capsizing like a ship as it hit the open air and plummeted. And the fire was everywhere now, raining down with the falling pieces, streaks of orange snaking across the sky.

"And that's when I saw the bodies. Two of them. They looked like rag dolls twisting in the air, but I knew they weren't. I knew they were people. I could mostly see them in silhouette, but I could tell that one wore a dress and one wore pants, so I figured it to be a man and woman. With everything moving at once, I didn't see where they fell from exactly – the tower, I guess - but it seemed like they were in the air forever. I guess time got slow on me just then. I don't know.

"I got that feeling, that acid taste you get in the back of your throat, when you realize that you are in the middle of this profound moment, yeah? Then after it happens, everything can be divided into before and after this moment. Forever. But right now you're in it. And you're powerless to affect it at all.

"And then the bodies descended out of view. The sky throbbed with light when the lightning struck again. I realized that I'd been holding my breath for some time, and when I inhaled, my chest spasmed a couple of times.

"I ran to where it seemed like the bodies fell, scrabbling up a part of the cliff face that wasn't as steep. As I got close I could hear the fire crackling. I could smell the burned smell all around me. I assumed it was coming from the top of the tower, but then I saw that there was another fire on the ground. It looked like it was contained – like someone had a bonfire going unrelated to all of this stuff going on.

"Anyway, I stepped up onto the plateau where the tower stood, and the girl's body was on the ground maybe 30 feet in front of me. I knew it couldn't be Amity, but that's all I could think as I got closer. Her face was turned away so I couldn't see much.

"And then something heavy thumped me on the back of the skull, and I was out."

He looks at me, and I realize I haven't moved in a long time. I've been sucked into this story, the images dancing in my head. I figure he's about to go on, but he just keeps on looking at me. I don't know what to do, so I clear my throat even though it's not necessary at all.

He exhales through his nostrils in a way that reminds me of a dog again, but a more aggressive breed this time. Not sure why he's staring me down like this. Glenn is an intense dude sometimes.

"When I woke, I was standing. My arms were bound, and I was blindfolded. I could still smell the ash in the air, so I knew the tower was near. I leaned a little to my right and felt something metal and sharp there against my leg. I had this sense that I was in a trap of some kind.

"I took a deep breath and waited. I listened. I couldn't hear much, though, except for fire crackling somewhere in the distance. I tried to reason out who would have done this to me or what the hell was going on, but I knew there was no way to make sense of it. This negativity just welled up in me - this total belief that I was trapped. Powerless.

"It's weird how if you believe you're defeated, you are. I was so certain that I had no control that it became real. And the only option I could see was flinging my body into the walls around me. Not even a real attempt at an escape, you know? Just an expression of despair."

He paws at his jaw a moment as he continues.

"So after that long moment of hesitation I hurled myself toward the trap, thrashing and kicking into that sharpness I felt to my right. Well, I fell over immediately. I guess it wasn't much of a trap after all. With my arms roped to my sides, I couldn't catch myself and just flopped teeth first onto the ground.

"Landing pulled the blindfold loose enough for me to see

some. First, I saw the tower not far off. Looking back, I'd been standing in a row of swords. There was nothing in front of me or behind me that whole time – just blades jammed into the ground to my left and right - but I threw myself directly into the swords like a goddamn fool. When I looked down at my arms, I saw how loose the bonds were. I pulled free with almost no effort."

He winces.

"I almost laughed at how ridiculous it all was. And then I felt this little prick of pain in my foot. My gaze swung over just in time to see the blood start gushing out. I guess one of the blades got me pretty good cause the front half of my foot was dangling. I think I was in shock or something cause it didn't hurt as bad as it should. I crawled to the bonfire and jammed my foot in to cauterize the wound. "

We're silent for a moment.

"Can you bleed to death there?" I say. "I mean, when that hooded man killed me I just came back here. No damage."

"I think it's different when you do what I did," he says. "I crossed over by walking into the light. Physically crossed over, you know? It's not the same as what happened to you. I mean, hell, just look at my foot. Seems pretty permanent to me."

"Yeah. Jesus. Good point, dude."

I can't help but look at his foot, and though it's covered by a slipper, I can see that stump in my mind.

"So wait," I say. "What about that belly wound? You were gut shot and healed yourself."

He squints.

"It's not exactly…"

His words trail off into a smile.

"Ah. But that would be telling," he says. "Anyhow, I'm more concerned with how we'll get back there to find Amity. Like we just talked about, taking the physical route has its risks."

We're quiet for a moment.

"I know what we can do," I say.

CHAPTER 9

The brown fluid glugs out of the bottle and splashes into the tumbler. For some reason the words "hair of the dog" pop into my head, though they don't apply here in any way. It's like the sight and smell and taste of alcohol conjure a bunch of booze jargon whether it applies or not.

Done pouring, Glenn sets the bottle down on the counter. With his hand out of the way, I get a better look at the red wax coating the neck of the bottle. A few streaks lay frozen in place where they ran down onto the body. They look like red rain on a windshield, like the wipers will come along any second to erase them. I take my glass as Glenn chugs from his.

The words "Kentucky Bourbon" play in my mind as I drink. I guess I read them on the bottle. It tastes exactly like every other bourbon I've ever had. I don't really understand the displays of state pride in these matters, but whatever.

To me, it tastes like something a doctor would give me in some dire situation. He'd grit his teeth and say, "This is our last hope," and hand me a glass of this.

I'm not sick, but I drink the medicine anyway. Of course, I would've been just as happy to mix this with a delicious cola or something, but Glenn kept going on and on about how smooth this bourbon is. He's a boastful man when it comes to his drinks, a beverage braggart. So the longer he goes on, the harder it gets to say, "It all tastes like fermented garbage water to me, dude. Let's mix it with some barrel aged Sam's Choice Cola for its robust flavor, premium carbonation, and syrupy mouth feel."

I drink again. My field of vision narrows to the tunnel leading to the bottom of the cup. I watch the ice cubes slosh around and clink into each other as the fluid ripples. Pretty sure Glenn said, "on the rocks," three times while he was getting the glasses around. Three times! Unreal.

"So what if this works for you and not for me?" he says.

I pull myself out of the tunnel, look at him, and blink. I give my brain a beat to try to catch the meaning, but I still don't get it.

"What?" I say.

"Well, I've had a few drinks plenty of times and never… crossed over or whatever," he says. "What if this is just happening to you?"

"Oh," I say. "Yeah, I don't know."

Glenn huffs. I drink. When I come up for air, he's still glaring at me.

"What do you want from me? I'm neither an expert on the rules of going to that place nor a drink-ologist," I say.

"Seems like you've got me on another of your goose chases," he says.

"Another? When did we chase geese before at my behest?"

He grumbles, but no discernible words come out before he cuts himself off with a slug of whiskey. I swear, Glenn is getting weirder by the day.

We drink a while, and we don't say much. The glasses rise and fall and clang on the counter. The ice cubes swirl and bash against the glass barriers encasing them. My fingers chill from holding the cup, but warmth rolls up and down the rest of me.

The liquor gurgles as it hits the back of my throat and falls into my stomach in a way that seems rough. Undignified. Glenn seems to be able to pull this off with more composure, but I at least match him drink for drink. It's not a total loss.

I can sort of sense the effects of the booze coming upon me. Weirdly, though it's a depressant, it seems to energize me. My eyes open a little wider, and I feel awake. My thoughts come out of the clouds and sharpen into focus. They start to wander.

And somehow the dilemma before me grows clear. If I've learned anything in my recent travels, it's that I don't think the physical realm can fulfill me... or maybe anyone. And yet I don't necessarily believe in anything beyond what's here and now. Even if I've had what felt like glimpses of something else, I don't know what they mean or what they really are.

So I'm left with a choice: I can try to accept that all that truly exists is the physical world and try to cope with the anxiety and dread that piles upon my existence since I know it can't satisfy me. Or I can choose to try to believe something unbelievable, which would be a lifelong effort and perhaps equally anxiety inducing.

I don't know. There may only be one thing I am sure of. Whichever path I choose, I will be disappointed.

Glenn clears his throat, and my mind snaps once more to my immediate surroundings. I'm drunk now. My face is warm.

Glenn's cheeks are flushed all red, and he looks a bit shiny, so I believe he's drunk as well. He keeps licking his lips.

"Well," he says.

That's it. He doesn't go on. He stares out at nothing.

Red on the Inside

My eyes trace down the tendrils of stem dangling from the plant hung over the sink. They seem so motionless. Even though we're inside, it feels like a breeze should pick up and swing them around or something.

I figure Glenn will eventually expound upon his aborted thought. Nope. He drinks. I hate to feel left out, so I follow suit.

We sit in the quiet. It's not unpleasant. It's tired in a way, but everything holds still better than usual. The world fails to overwhelm me the way it sometimes does. It doesn't squirm and twist around me anymore. It just lies there, barely breathing, perhaps asleep.

Apart from the hum of the fluorescent bulb above, it might be peaceful, even. I'm not quite sure.

That burst of alcohol fueled energy erodes with a quickness, and the depressant qualities begin to take hold. I can feel it in my eyelids first. It's not a heaviness so much as a tightness - the sense that the corners of my eyes can't open all the way, even if I stretch them.

And then sounds feel a little farther away. I can still hear everything, but the noises transpire way outside of me now, somehow dampened. It doesn't get to me the same way. It's like someone turned up the plate reverb and now everything is sitting further back in the mix, all wet and smooth. Except for my thoughts, that is. They're dry and bright and right up front.

Even so, the calm cranks up. It's that sad calm that I've been feeling a lot lately, the kind that saps the energy out of everything, but now it's intensified.

And I'm stuck inside myself, and I can feel the wind suck in and out of me and my chest puff up and collapse, and the air scrapes over the back of my throat, and the dry forms cracks in my lips, and my tongue is all coarse like it belongs in some lizard's mouth. The distance between me and everything else just grows and grows.

But I don't mind, really. I guess that's the benefit of falling into this particular hole. It seems like it's all just as well. What's the difference, yeah?

Yeah.

Yeah.

So what?

I blink a few times like that might change all of this somehow. It doesn't. It just reinforces how odd my eyelids feel and how dry my eyes are. I picture the whites webbed with the red of blood vessels.

I drink some more. And some more again.

And it occurs to me that before long I'll be too fucked to move, which is also just as well. There's nowhere to go anyway. There's nothing to tell you. There's no one to tell.

There's nothing.

Nothing but the minutes and hours and days getting sucked down the drain.

Glenn jerks forward in his chair, forcing me to remember that he's still there. I realize he put on aviator sunglasses at some point, and they make him look a lot like a mustached John Goodman. He gasps, and his feet snap to shoulder width. It's somewhat of a defensive position, as though he's bracing to lose his balance, which generally is difficult to do while sitting in a chair but not impossible.

"It's happening," he says.

CHAPTER 10

"It's happening," Glenn says again.

His voice is quiet with some grit to it, so it sounds pretty important. Even so, I try to think of what he must be referring to and can't. I look around the room. The only thing happening is nothing.

"Oh, shit," he says and brings his fist to his mouth. "You were right."

My lips purse to ask what the hell he is talking about, but I scan the room one more time first in case I somehow missed something. Everything looks to be conveying the same motionlessness as before. However, my eyes cross or something as they move over the far wall. There's a blur in that area that even squinting won't erase. I rub at my eyelids a second, but it's still there.

Wait.

It's not a blur. It's the other world, a smudged version of it, anyway.

"Do you see it?" he says, batting at my shoulder.

"Yeah. I see it," I say.

"Well, good," he says. "Good."

We sit and look at the blur for a moment, though whether or not we're seeing the same thing, I couldn't say.

I can't really tell what I'm looking at. It's all out of focus, but I think I see some trees.

"So what do we do now?" he says.

Good question. Damn. This guy is good.

"I don't know," I say.

I think about it a moment before I go on, and I rub the back of my fingers over my chapped lips.

"Maybe if we drank more we'd cross over all the way?" I say.

Glenn's eyebrows go up, and even through the aviators, I can see his eyes open up real wide for a second like he just saw Jacob Marley shaking some chains in his face. He turns toward me.

"Grobnagger," he says, his voice half gasping. "Yes! It's freaking brilliant, man. We will drink our way there."

I can't remember him saying the word "freaking" before, but it makes me laugh for some reason. When I look over, Glenn is laughing, too, and that makes me laugh harder, I guess in part because I doubt we're even laughing at the same thing.

Mid chuckle, he tips the bottle and more whiskey gurgles into our glasses. He doesn't stop pouring in time, and the overflow spills all over the counter. We both stop laughing as the flood of booze washes onto a pile of mail.

Glenn wheezes like a man that has just been shot.

"Oopsie," he says.

We laugh more. His mouth looks all juicy again, like a weird, wet John Goodman maw. This freaks me out, and I can't take my eyes off of the laughing hole in his face.

It's weird how gross it is to be alive in a way. Saliva and snot and mucus coming out every which way. The jagged bones in every mouth going ever darker yellow unless the owners pay

58

people to smear bleach around in there. Breath wafting the stink from inside until the whole world smells like dried spit.

I don't know. Maybe I'm just drunk.

I drink again. I realize that it doesn't taste like anything anymore. It's just a stinging tingle draining down the tube to my stomach. This whole drinking process seems tedious at this point. It seems like there'd be a better way to ingest this, but then I guess that's probably what those high school kids were thinking a few towns over when they injected Jack Daniels into their veins and died.

I refocus on the wall across the room, and the blur is a touch less smudged looking. Translucent trees stand before me on a sparsely wooded hill. These images sort of look like they're being displayed on the wall by a projector with a bulb that's about to die, but it's at least a little brighter than it was before.

And the air I breathe feels and smells and tastes differently now. It's fresh and a little humid. The odors of outside and plant life and dirt enter my nostrils.

Glenn giggles, and looking his way, I see that he's slipped his sandals off to put his feet into the scraggle of grass and dead leaves that are becoming visible above the tiled floor. Even when it's half see-through like it is, the green is striking. Watching his toes wiggle, I remember how cold it felt to trudge through this stuff back when I moved through the mist toward the tree. I feel a weird tingle in my shoulder like I'm about to shiver, but I don't.

I lick my lips, but they're too dry to help at this point. It's like licking the Grand Canyon. Glenn keeps making noises I guess I would call cooing. He sounds like a cross-eyed baby that's trying to wrap his fat fingers around a block.

59

I drink a little and watch this fool swish his feet around in the grass. His mouth hangs ajar in a smile like one of those slack-jawed weirdos that can only grin with their uvula on full display. You'd think that quality would have been bred out of humanity by now.

Nope.

More like survival of the dimmest.

And as I watch the man dip his toes into the green, the fundamental difference between me and Glenn occurs to me by way of metaphor. Glenn lives his life like everything is music, and I live my life like everything is words.

Music is immediate. It never stops to think about itself. It lives in a moment, and for all it knows, each moment is infinite. It doesn't worry about whether or not this particular song will end. It doesn't examine itself or its existence. It doesn't reflect. It just is.

Words are always one step removed from the moment, though. They detach and describe the moment to themselves. They can only reflect.

So Glenn looks out at the world for what it is, but I look inside to try to make sense of the outside with words. He simply is, while I am reflections of reflections of reflections. I am layer upon layer of self awareness that never ends. I never stop thinking about myself. I am never immediate, never purely in the moment.

Always partially detached.

Always partially withdrawn.

I go back into my cup for a second, and when I come up for air, something is different. I stare at Glenn for a long moment before it hits me. He is now translucent as well. He's like a ghost kicking his feet in some grass. Something about his posture and jerky motions make me think of a toddler thrashing his legs in a kiddie pool, except it'd be a see-through, ghost toddler, I guess. Sounds like a terrible horror movie.

"Holy shit," I say.

Glenn does a double take. He rips off the aviators to look around.

"Cripes," he says.

Again, the word "cripes" seems funny just now. I laugh. I don't know. Perhaps it's this intoxication thing.

My eyes close as I chuckle, and out of the blue, Louise pops into my head. I remember sitting on the couch with her legs draped over my lap, watching TV. The heat emanated off of her. She was one of those perpetually warm people, like a broken radiator that you can never turn down. I'm the opposite. I'm always cold with icy fingers that make everyone recoil, but she made it go away. She warmed everything up.

And I remember that. I remember feeling safe and warm.

But I open my eyes, and now my nose is all cold, and I'm drunk as hell, and I'm laughing at nothing.

"Shit. I'm crossed over now," Glenn says. "So drink up, Grobs. We got shit to take care of."

I take the bottle straight to my face and guzzle the rest down. At least I'm good at one thing.

CHAPTER 11

The booze gurgles about in my gut and attacks my liver and works its way up to kill some more brain cells. It's all for a good cause, though. A damn good cause.

I watch a hazy Glenn tromp around the woods while I await my turn at the weirdness. His mouth hangs open still, a dumb smile gaping out at the other world as he moves around there. He walks through the kitchen wall during this process and makes his way up the hill, which is not as weird to watch as it probably sounds. I've seen it all before and shit.

Meanwhile, the alcohol seeps into my bloodstream and continues its creep up toward my head. I can't feel these particular bodily functions transpire. I merely feel the slow and steady escalation of my drunkenness. I'm getting to that point where I keep getting dumber and slower and sadder. Alcohol is a depressant after all. It's depressing itself on my brain bits and squeezing the serotonin and stuff out so all that's left is the sad juice.

But it's all good, yeah? Soon I'll be in another place, checking out some mystical woods and shit, staggering around with Glenn, possibly even hanging out with Amity. She seems cool as hell, too. I mean, who else would go out into that crazy place and try to live there? Who else would throw the whole world away to try to understand a place that can't be understood? I think that's pretty awesome somehow.

I mean, is it desperate? Of course it is. But we're all going to die, you know? We only have so long to try to do anything that means something to us. I think it's cool that she just goes for it. It's desperate, but the honest kind of desperate that makes sense. Some amount of urgency is a good thing, I say.

My eyes focus on Glenn in the distance as he leans against a tree at the top of the hill. After watching him a second, it occurs to me that he looks solid again. And so does the tree. I look around. The woods about me look opaque. It's the kitchen wall that I can see through now.

I stand and wobble a second, and there's a faint tingle in the backs of my knees. Taking a step forward, I realize how drunk I really am. My feet are dumb. My legs are dumber. My top half wants to flop about like a rag doll. My neck seems to lack interest in holding my head up. It goes through the motions, but you can tell its heart's not in it, so my skull lolls around as I walk.

My body is the worst.

"All right, Grobs," Glenn says. "Welcome over."

He removes his shoulder from the tree and stands with his arms folded across his chest. His legs are well past shoulder width apart, so he looks like he's standing like a super hero or something. I laugh. He laughs, too. Apparently, he doesn't really need a reason for laughter at this point. I guess the laughs come cheaply once you kill a significant enough portion of your mind. Good to know.

I follow a path beaten into the grass that leads up to where Glenn stands on the hilltop. As I ascend, I note that this hill is steeper than it looks from afar. With my motor skills diminished, it's a struggle to mount the damn thing. My head flops indifferently on my wet noodle neck. Glenn laughs more.

What fun, what fun. What a goddamn delight life is.

I kick and scratch and paw at the path to work my way up, but my eyes stay locked on Glenn's dumb head, bobbling atop his body in a fit of laughter. What a jolly motherfucker he turned out to be this afternoon, shaking like a bowlful of jelly and everything.

"Laugh it up," I say.

After I say it, I realize that I didn't speak the words so much as yell them as loud as my vocal cords could muster, my voice breaking up into that rasped out half yell, half scream thing. That vocal delivery always reminds me of some jungle predator about to kill something in a documentary.

"Whoa," Glenn says, dabbing his fingertips at his brow. "Chill, Grobnagger."

Chill?

Chill.

Unbelievable. He stopped laughing, which is something. Maybe I should be thankful that he didn't tell me to take a chill pill.

"I'll chill," I say.

Again, I don't realize the bitter sarcasm I'm employing until I hear the words coming out of my mouth. I feel like I never realize how angry I am until it's vomiting every which way.

Glenn doesn't say anything. He just looks at the ground.

I get to the top of the hill and return to a semi-upright posture, and Glenn turns so that we're standing just about shoulder to shoulder looking out over the other side of the hill. The trees seem to grow thicker from here until they turn to fully fledged woods a little ways on.

Up on high, the air seems brighter somehow. I don't know what that means exactly, but that's how it feels. Deal with it. I have a feeling that won't be the case up ahead. It seems darker up there somehow. I don't know. I might just be shitfaced.

"Now what?" I say.

Glenn scratches under his eye.

"I kind of figured we'd just follow this path," he says.

My eyes trace along the lines where the grass gives way to the dirt walkway under my feet.

"Makes sense," I say.

"Then let's roll," he says.

I follow him downhill. The slope on this side is more gradual, which is nice. The words "leisurely stroll" spring to mind. A little embarrassing, but I will try to remember to not tell anyone that this thought happened, so it should be fine.

I take in Glenn's sloppy gait, however, and I realize that there's nothing leisurely about this after all. He stumbles and bumbles, his legs seemingly drunker than the rest of him, and I guess I must be doing something similar. I look down at my legs, watch them jerk and buckle and sway over the terrain.

Yep.

What a pair of idiots we are.

We move into the woods before long, and tree roots pock the path with their gnarled bits poking up from the Earth. It's a matter of time before one of us trips, I'm certain.

Also, I was totally right. The air doesn't feel as bright down here. It's like a dark wind right in my face. Total bullshit.

"Air is dark," I say, not necessarily meaning to say this out loud.

"What?" Glenn says.

I repeat it all pissed off like he's an idiot.

"THE AIR," I say. "IS DARK."

He doesn't say anything, but I can see the faintest smile curl the corners of his lips, and yet again I can't tear my eyes away from that juicy, disgusting hole in his face he calls a mouth. Yeah, smile away, you dumb son of a bitch. Smile for miles and miles at what a delight it all is, you pussy motherfucker.

OK.

OK.

Wow. Calm down, Grobs.

I make a concerted effort to unclench my jaw, and I feel all the muscles all around my temples let go in unison. I take a deep breath. The pressure in my head dies down a little further.

Red heat pulses in my cheeks. I don't know anything about blood pressure numbers, but I bet right now the gauge would read, "1,000," over "Holy Shit!"

I close my eyes and take another deep breath. My toe kicks at a root, but it doesn't hit squarely enough to trip me. See? Not everything is awful.

Just almost everything.

Glenn steps on a stick, and the crunch and snap pulls me out of my head a little. I remember where we are and what we're doing. We're here to find Amity. She doesn't want to leave here probably, but we're going to talk to her anyhow if we can find her before the alcohol wears off.

Like I said before, it's a damn good cause.

Amity. She's an interesting girl, yeah? I remember reading her journal, and though I can't call most of the specifics to mind just now, I remember she was scared of a man. She was scared that he knew things. She was scared to even write down his name. That seems important, right?

"You think it was Farber?" I say.

I watch Glenn's eyes return from dazed to alert.

"What?" he says.

"I said 'Do you think it was Farber?'" I say.

"Huh?" he says. "What are you talking about?"

"Riston Farber," I say. "Stands about yay high. Shaved head. Hovers spoons like a goddamn champion. Possible murderer and returner from the dead."

"I know who Farber is," he says. "I don't know what the hell you're talking about."

Hm… Did I forget to explain something?

"Um…" I say. "Farber. Something about Farber. Oh, do you think he was the guy Amity was scared of? In her journal, I mean?"

Glenn scoffs.

"Amity would have no reason to be scared of Riston Farber," he says. "Trust me on that."

His soggy lips curl up again. He's such a smug bastard sometimes.

"You sound awfully sure, but you've been wrong about shit before. Seems to me that the guy came back from the dead," I say. "And he tried to assassinate me, for shit's sake. I wouldn't be so quick to take him all lightly."

"Thing is, he did neither of those things," he says. "He's all smoke and mirrors, Grobnagger. He ain't nothing to be scared of."

"That's bold talk for a guy with half of a foot," I say. "You know so much you got your toes lopped off. You were wrong

67

then, and you're wrong now. Just think about that. Farber tried to kill me. I heard the glass break and saw the bullet holes in the door. How is that smoke and mirrors?"

It occurs to me that Glenn is no longer walking. I stop and turn back to him to find his face the color of hatred itself, which it turns out is a deep shade of red with just a hint of a purple hue in certain areas. His jowls quiver. His demon eyes lock onto mine, and I can feel them looking through me.

The aviators are gone. They cannot help me now.

"Farber didn't do that," he says, through gritted teeth. "He's a phony."

"How do you know? You act like you know it all, but you don't make any sense," I say. "I mean, if Farber didn't try to kill me, who did?"

His lip curls.

"I did it," he says. "It was a trick, just like one of Farber's bullshit illusions. I had to do it. I had to get you on board for finding Amity, so I made it look like…"

But I don't hear any more of the words coming out of that cock holster he calls a mouth. I just watch those dumbass lips flap in total fucking silence for another millisecond, and then I'm on him.

As my fists loop in a flurry of overhand rights and hooks that connect with his face and neck, some detached part of me is concerned. See, I don't remember deciding to do this. It is just happening. I'm just pummeling his face in without consciously saying, "Yeah, let's do that."

I guess for once I'm in the moment.

He's either too drunk or too dumb to get his hands up to block my combinations. To his credit, however, he does backpedal, bob and lean away from the punches enough to make some of the blows glance off. Probably some instinct leftover from his boxing days. Anyway, I'm throwing pretty wildly, so most swings don't connect with full force. Some are close enough, though.

I finally land a clean shot right on his mouth. The sound is part crack, part slap, part thud, and weirdly wet. He totters backward, leaning further and further back like a tree getting chopped down, but before I see him land, I'm down, too, in a flash.

Straight down. Flat on my face.

Did he somehow get me, and I never saw it coming? My mind races to replay the last few seconds.

No. He didn't hit me.

I tripped on a root.

The moment of confusion snaps me out of my murderous rage somewhat, anyway, and we both stay put, a good 7 or 10 feet apart from each other, breathing all heavy through open mouths like dogs in the summer.

After a while, I get my wind back and sit up. I swivel myself so my shoulders are pointed away from him, but I can still keep an eye on him out of the corner of my eye. I don't want to kill his face anymore, but I'd rather not look at him much just yet.

I am drunk. It is hard to think right. But apparently Glenn tricked me. He made me think someone was trying to kill me. He lied to me this whole time.

Shit. I don't know. This guy was supposed to be my friend, right? Maybe my only friend.

And by now the rage is long gone. Numb takes its place. It feels like someone pulled out the cork or something and all of my feelings are leaking out, like all of my nerves are severed now, like all the pieces are shattered.

"Why?" I say.

At first he remains quiet. I shoot a glance his way. His face is angled away from me, but I can see some bruises on his cheek starting to show. A thoughtful look occupies his features. He clears his throat and speaks:

"The human brain is a funny piece of work, Grobnagger," he says. "It fools itself time and again. It sees what it expects to see. It's sort of like how detectives get tunnel vision for one suspect or one story to explain a crime, and then they start seeing all the evidence in whatever way necessary to support their story, even if it's wrong. They see all the data from the angle of what they expected to see, and they ignore the pieces that don't seem to fit."

He bats a hand at his chest, I guess to brush some dust off.

"So if I plant the suggestion properly, you'll see the reality I want you to see, because subconsciously you already expect it."

I feel the air suck into my lungs and realize that I've held my breath during his speech.

I should say something. Right? It feels like I should definitely say something.

"So you hypnotized me or something?" I say.

"Something like that," he says. "Another of my parlor tricks. I can't make people do things they don't want to do or anything like that, but I can kind of flash them into a suggestible state for a few seconds, influence how they'll see certain things. When you were in a suggestible state, I told you you'd hear broken glass and see bullet holes. All I had to do was bust up the door pretty good and throw a rock through the window, and your brain saw what it expected to see."

"Dude. That seems like a dick move," I say.

No regard at all for my security deposit, but I guess that should surprise me least of all.

And still I feel nothing. Am I in shock? How has the anger abandoned me so rapidly? It seems like I should be more pissed than this. I turn it over a few times, feeling around my various brain parts to see if I'm pissed deep down somewhere, but I think I'm not. It's just a dead sensation inside. Nothing else.

It's weird.

Glenn plucks a tall piece of grass gone to seed from the ground and rubs the stem back and forth between his fingers, so it spins super fast. His eyes don't leave the twirling plant as he speaks.

"Do you actually regret getting involved, though?" he says. "Would you rather you sat alone in your cell all this time instead of helping me find my girl?"

For a second I think he means I'd somehow still be stuck in the cell in the basement of the League's empty hospital, but then I realize he means I'd be home alone in my apartment. I guess it was my cell in a lot of ways.

I was a single-celled creature.

I'm not anymore.

"I guess not," I say.

He turns his head so his eyes face toward the sky. I see now that his right eye is swollen just about shut. I guess I got him better than I thought. After he stares out there for what seems like a long time, he nods.

"I figured as much," he says.

We sit still a while. It's quiet.

And the air out here feels dark as hell.

CHAPTER 12

In time we gather ourselves and walk some more. Deeper in the woods, the shade grows a touch thicker, but there's little else of note to report.

No Amity. No nothing. Just a bullshit waste of time like every other damn thing.

We walk a little further on the path, and Glenn grunts something I can't understand. I realize quickly, however, that he didn't say any words. It was the sound of him heaving. I am able to deduce this when he leans over to puke all over some ferns.

I stand aside when the man "upchucks" as he would say. The real world is beginning to fade back in some for me. It's blurry and see-through, but I remember how it all faded out with great quickness last time.

Glenn rights himself, and I rejoin him.

"We might need to bring some booze with us or something next time," I say. "I mean, if we're going to make this work, we'll need to stay drunk longer."

Glenn smirks and vomits some more as if to point out what a bad idea that would be. I can't say that he puked on cue like that to make a point, but it sure worked out that way.

A well-timed barf is worth a thousand words.

So this plan kind of sucked as it turns out. The only things we accomplished were a one sided fist fight and a lot of idiocy. I guess I also learned that everything everyone says is a stupid lie.

Yay.

I realize too late that I'm standing a touch close to Glenn's spray this time. Some of his vomit spatters onto my shoes, and that's enough for me. I retch.

And what seems like gallons of regurgitated bourbon flows through the grass on this heavenly plane.

It is brown. Pretty foamy.

I lie on my bed, my own bed in my not so dangerous apartment. It seems darker here. The street lights shined into Glenn's living room so it felt like the world never really went all the way to sleep. My bedroom blocks out everything. The world might as well be dead outside of this room for all I can tell. Tonight I will sleep under cover of the black nothing for the first time in several weeks.

The drunk wore off some time ago, but I still feel dead on the inside. Ever since the fight, I've felt nothing. Maybe there's some sense of disappointment in there, but it's pretty faint, I think.

After the vomiting session, we gave up. We sat down in the brush and let the real world fade back in around us. Nobody said much. We came back around on someone's patio a couple blocks from Glenn's house.

It wasn't until we made our way back to Glenn's that I realized that I could just go home now. I could sleep in my own bed. Glenn didn't object. He didn't say anything. So I packed up my cat, and here we are. Mardy is asleep at the foot of the bed. I can't see him, but I can feel him there near my feet.

Red on the Inside

Apparently the maintenance man fixed the door and window and cleaned up all of the glass at some point. Will I get a bill for that? I'm not sure how this works.

Anyway, I am back to where I started. Alone in my cell. Will I find a good reason to leave this time or nah?

The alcohol made me feel much worse, at least. The lining of my stomach burns, and liquid keeps sloshing around in my gut, so that'll need to rocket out of my ass in a violent spray eventually. Good times.

Even with the physical ailments, on some level it feels pretty great to be back. It's better than I thought it'd be. Being apart from everyone fills me with such relief. I remember now why I always liked it so much. It smells like home. It feels like home. My body uncoils like all of my muscles can unclench for once, and I can let all of my weight rest on the bed, as limp as a wet towel. Never underestimate the pleasure of letting yourself be dead weight for a while. Being completely idle is underrated, I'd say.

And it occurs to me that maybe I haven't changed a bit despite all that's happened. Maybe I do prefer my cell to whatever the hell kind of freedom exists out there in the real world. Maybe I just want to be left alone, like I said all along.

Maybe.

Is this it? Is this what life is? Does no one ever really change or grow? Do we just spin in place for the duration of our lives and fool ourselves into believing that we're becoming something new every so often?

I roll over, and pull the blanket up over my shoulders so the edge rests on my top lip. My eyes open for a moment. I can see nothing in the dark, but I can feel the sting of the tired in them whenever my eyelids move.

It will feel so good just to turn everything all the way off for a while.

I'm in the woods again in my dreams. I'm on the move, too, moving away from the path. I don't know why, but this seems the way to go. I bend a branch of thorns out of my way and press forward into the foliage.

The green mess of plant life surrounds me. Leaves shake. Vines dangle, twisted around tree branches. The light spills out of the sky in the ever shifting gaps in the canopy of leaves above, the spots of illumination seeming to constantly slide across the ground as the air moves branches all about.

And I realize that Amity has been talking to me this whole time. I hear her voice, but I can't make sense of her words. It's different from before, though. I can hear everything she says. It just doesn't make sense. I can't even hold on to fragments of it in my mind long enough to repeat them. Her words just drift past like the wind.

I can tell she is talking to me. Just me. And she is not scared. I can read that much in her tone.

She is an interesting creature. Even though I can't understand what she's saying, I feel like I know her a little bit just hearing her voice. She is smart and quiet and focused in an unusual way. She talks slowly, seeming to choose her words carefully, though they mean nothing to me.

She seems like the kind of person that you'd lean toward whenever she started talking so you wouldn't miss anything. She seems like the kind of person that has no sense of how entertaining she is.

But I know more than her sound, I guess. I know she is out here by choice.

And I know she wants something more. More than McDonald's and sitcoms and video games and movies and money and sex and all of it, all of the things the physical world has to offer. She wants more than that.

And I like that.

CHAPTER 13

The sidewalk stretches out into the distance, and I stomp my way toward the horizon. Cars rumble past on the street, all of the engine sounds combining into a drone that makes it seem quiet to me somehow, quieter than actual silence. It's weird how that works. Constant noise always has a weird privacy to it, too, like no one could possibly notice me among all of this loudness.

My head throbs with that morning after headache. I took some ibuprofen, but so far the headache remains. It's not too bad, at least.

I cut through the grass as I round off the last corner, and there's Glenn's house up ahead. The red door stands out even from a distance. I smear my palms against my pant legs.

I've made this trek enough times now that it feels a little like going home in a lot of ways. So why am I nervous?

I hesitate at the door. I swallow in dry throat, and I can distinctly feel that lump shift, my Adam's apple or whatever. I knock.

I hear something thumping on the other side of the door, and then it opens. Glenn squints at me from the shade inside of the house. After a beat, I realize it's only one eye that's squinting. Is that weird? Seems like a weird face to make, right? Is that aggressive, or…? When he leans into the light, the purple shade of his bruises refreshes my memory.

That's right. I sort of bashed his face in a little bit. Perhaps that's why I was nervous on the way here. So he wasn't squinting at me. His eye is swollen into a perpetual squint for the time being.

"So you're knocking now?" he says.

I look at the concrete step underfoot.

"Well, yeah I guess so," I say.

"You don't have to do that, Grobnagger," he says. "We've traversed the astral plane together, buddy. That's a lasting bond. My casa is your casa. My Oreos are your Oreos. Apart from the Double Stufs, at least. Those are mine."

He steps out of the doorway, but I'm still hesitant to step through. I consider apologizing for the face pummeling, but I decide against it.

"Come on in," he says.

I pass through the doorway and stand in the foyer. It takes a second for my eyes to adjust to being out of direct sunlight. Glenn closes the door behind me.

"You hungry?" he says.

That's one of the things I like about Glenn. He always knows exactly what to say.

We sit at the snack bar, shoveling food into our mouth parts. It's a typical day at Glenn's house, really, except the sun seems extra bright. It slants in through the window, lighting a rectangle that stretches across the countertop and onto the wall. Somehow the light isn't harsh, though. It's pleasant.

Glenn takes a big bite of waffle and then talks with his mouth full.

"Thing is, drinking our way there is just as dangerous as going the direct route," he says. "In terms of the injuries being permanent, anyway. Just take a look at my face if you want an exhibit A on that assertion."

Awkward.

I start to reply:

"Yeah. Listen, I'm sorry about the-"

But Glenn interrupts:

"Forget it," he says. "It's nothing. We were drunk. Drunk folks resort to fisticuffs with some regularity as a rule. Way I see it, it could have been worse. I'm glad one of us didn't snap an ankle on a tree root or some goddamn thing. I say we're lucky. This won't cause us any problems. It will heal."

I consider suggesting he heal his face the way he healed that gut shot, but I don't want to push it. He's not pissed about me using his face as a piñata? Great. I'm not about to mess that up.

He opens the waffle iron and pops out a fresh waffle that's all golden brown. My mouth gets all wet just looking at a well caramelized piece of breakfast confection like that.

"You want another one?" he says.

I think about this for about one millionth of a second.

"Well, yeah," I say.

He smiles, and the skin around his puffy eye wrinkles all weird. His face looks like a half-finished special effects makeup from a boxing movie. I should remember to not tell him that, though.

He plops the waffle onto my plate and hands it back.

"You tried that birch syrup yet?" he says, pointing an elbow vaguely in the direction of the assortment of syrup bottles off to one side of the counter.

"Not yet," I say.

"It's kind of interesting," he says. "I mean, I wouldn't want it all the time, but it's a unique flavor. I'm glad I got it."

"I'll give it a go," I say.

The birch syrup looks pretty well indistinguishable from the various maple varieties here. I pop the top open and take a smell. It's somewhat subtle, but the aroma reminds me of caramel with just a touch of spice.

I'm intrigued.

I pour a decent amount into my syrup cup. (Glenn insists that you use less syrup and achieve superior flavor if you use a small syrup container and dip each bite rather than pouring the syrup directly onto the waffle or pancake or French toast ahead of time where much of it gets soaked up. As usual when it comes to matters of cuisine, he couldn't be more right. The man is a hero to me. I honestly can't stress that enough. He is a hero.)

I dip and taste. Perhaps interesting was the right word for it after all. It's like syrup with a faint chemical flavor mixed in. I don't know. It's pretty complex. Maybe I'd like it more if I had it a few times. Right now my palate is somewhat befuddled.

We eat some more, and the talking dies down for a time. The sunlight continues to shine with an abnormal brightness, so I watch Glenn's shadow stuff its face with shadow waffle on the wall. This is entertaining somehow.

It's weird how much something like the sun can affect us, though. It feels nice in here, even with a dull headache and hangover. Like here in the bright sunlight, it's just exciting to be alive. Maybe it's partially the endorphins from eating delicious food, but I'm thankful to be here.

"So what are we going to do?" Glenn says. "I mean, the drinking thing is out, obviously. You got any other ideas?"

"I've been thinking about that," I say. "You have any dreams last night?"

His eyes rotate toward the ceiling as he thinks about it.

"No," he says. "I had a hard time getting to sleep. Last time I looked at the clock it was after 4 am. I don't remember any dreams, though."

"Well, I had a dream," I say. "I was back in the woods, and I could hear Amity again."

Glenn gets all quiet. He licks his lips.

"She seemed safe," I say. "She wasn't scared."

"What did she say?" he says.

"I don't know," I say. "I couldn't make sense of it. I don't know if she was talking nonsense or my sleep brain couldn't concentrate on it properly, but I didn't understand her."

His lips press into each other and wiggle a few times, which kind of makes him look like a rodent, I think. I guess he's thinking about this.

"Well," he says. "I don't see how it helps us any more than it did last time."

With his eyes closed, he presses his index finger into his good eyelid and rubs at it.

"Do you?" he says.

"Maybe. I think she is pulling us over there," I say. "She can connect to us when we're sleeping somehow."

"That probably makes sense, but how do we use it?" he says.

"Well, when we're asleep, we can connect to her, but we're not in the right frame of mind to do anything with it, yeah?" I say. "What if it's like I said, and it has something to do with our brains being sort of asleep?"

"Could be," he says.

"Maybe there's a way to fight that," I say. "Like if you could drink a bunch of coffee and then fall asleep maybe. I mean, I know you don't want to mix an upper and a downer together necessarily. That messes with your heart, but maybe there's some way to do something like that safely, a way to fall asleep while our minds are fully alert."

Glenn stares out into the distance, his shoulders tilted away from me. He mumbles something half under his breath, so quiet I almost miss it entirely.

"What?" I say.

"Hypnosis," he says. "Sort of."

CHAPTER 14

The coffee machine gurgles, slurps, drips, suddenly wet with life. I watch the first few droplets develop into a trickle and then a full on stream of caffeinated dream juice. I'm still not totally clear on how we're going to drink this and then sleep. Either way, it smells tremendous.

Glenn dries his hands on a towel draped through a cabinet handle above the sink. He turns toward me, his eyes fixed on the pair of cardboard boxes on the countertop between us. He looks at them for a split second before he rips open one of the boxes and pulls the instruction leaflet out.

I already forget what these things are called, but they're some kind of sleep aid machines or something, whatever that might entail. I just followed Glenn around the sketchiest aisles at Meijer to find the damn things. I still don't know what they have to do with hypnosis either. I asked. Glenn just grunted unintelligible responses. He was in no mood to talk, I guess. His eyes looked all manic.

I rotate the open box so I can read the front. Apparently it's a "Nightwave Sleep Assistant Nw-102." Peeking inside, the device itself looks to be a black plastic box a little wider than a deck of cards. There's a decal on the front depicting a starry night and some kind of rolling hills or something. An LED bulb sits in a hole punched into the middle of the front of the box.

The bulb looks blue.

"How does this thing work?" I say, turning the box over in my hands.

Glenn holds up a finger at me, his nose hovers about two inches away from the instructions. His eyes flick from side to side like they're in fast forward as he reads.

"It's a pulsing light," he says, his voice all far away and distracted. "You lie in the dark with your eyes open and adjust your breathing to the time of the light. It slows down, and the light fading to dark fools your brain into thinking it's your eyelids drooping closed."

I think this over.

"That sounds pretty weird, dude," I say.

There's a pause before he answers, his eyeballs still flicking away.

"It's basically to help anxious people get to sleep without their swirl of thoughts and worries getting in the way," he says. "They just focus on the light and sort of trick their body into thinking they're already going into the physiological steps of sleep. I think there's a hypnotic quality to the process. I've always wanted to test them out, but I've never had a problem getting to sleep. Now we have the perfect reason to give them a shot."

"I guess that makes sense," I say. "So they actually work?"

"Not for everyone," he says. "It doesn't click for certain people. But for most people, it works great."

I nod even though I know he's not looking at me. I watch him read a while.

The coffee machine chokes out that stuttering, throaty sound as the brewing process comes to its end. I saw that Glenn opened a new bag. Some kind of extra dark roast. Based on the smell filling the room, it's going to be delicious. The smell is kind of earthy, and it reminds me of chocolate, too, somehow.

I look down at the little black box in my hand, spin it around a couple more times and hold it up.

"How did you even hear about these things?" I say.

He looks up at me for the first time in this conversation. For a full a second his eyes stare into mine with about as much blankness in them as a human expression can muster. Then he blinks a couple of times, and I can sort of see my question register.

"Oh, I saw Dr. Oz recommend them on TV," he says.

The blanket tumbles down onto my face, filling my field of vision with navy blue and white stripes.

"Hang on," I say.

I flop the edge of it around until I regain my grip, lifting the blanket back over my head once I do. I press it flat against the trim above the window while Glenn stretches duct tape along its edge and adheres the bedcover there. The roll of tape screeches as he pulls out a second layer of gummy gray stuff, tears it off, and swipes it into place with his fingertips, then presses the heel of his hand all along it to seal it up good.

I can't help but wonder what any passersby would think if they saw two grown men duct taping blankets over the guest bedroom windows in the middle of the day. Meth lab? Grow room for marijuana? Nope. Nothing weird like that. We're just astral projecting, dude. That's all.

"So the curtains wouldn't be enough, huh?" I say, stepping out of the way.

Glenn shakes his head as he tapes the left side of the blanket down in similar fashion. No need to double up on the tape here, though.

"Nah," he says. "It's too damn sunny today. We need it as dark as possible in here for these lights to work right. We need absolute blackness, if possible."

He turns to the other side and slaps some tape up there as well, and then we repeat the process on the other window with a tattered bedspread.

Even with the door open into the sunlit hallway, it's already pretty dim in here. I feel around until my fingers find my coffee mug sitting on the nightstand and take a sip.

This is coffee number three. The dark roast is delicious - everything I'd hoped it'd be, sure - but drinking three of these babies in rapid succession makes my throat feel all scorched and raw and gross somehow. And I know as I drink a couple more, the lining of my stomach is up next on the list of things to feel like they're on fire.

This is a small price to pay, however, for a chance to find Amity. I don't mean to complain. Glenn said we should try to finish two pots before we make our way toward the dream world, and I'm down to do my best toward achieving that goal.

I follow Glenn out into the hallway, the sudden snap to brightness overwhelming my pupils for a moment. We move toward the other end of the house.

"I kind of figured we'd each set up our own rooms," he says. "I thought about pulling my recliner into the guest room and using that – thing's like a damn nap machine – but after giving it some thought, I figure isolation to be best. No chance of distracting each other. No chance of my lights interfering with your lights or our breathing being in different rhythms and messing each other up or anything like that, you know?"

"Makes sense," I say.

He tosses me a quilted bedspread with pink and blue rectangles all over it, and we go to work taping blankets over the windows in Glenn's room as well. The process mostly resembles what we did in the guest room, but the windows in the master bedroom are quite a bit wider. On the first window, the tape holding the top left corner keeps pulling free before we can get the top right corner. It's kind of a bitch.

We anchor the tops of both blankets in time, though, and I chug a coffee while Glenn secures the sides.

Yep. I was right.

A small grease fire smolders in the center of my abdomen where my stomach used to be.

CHAPTER 15

I lie in the dark for a few seconds, my thumb tickling around the edges of the button on the plastic box clenched in my hand. For some reason, though I'm a little excited to see what Dr. Oz's sleep box is all about, I'm reluctant to actually press this thing. I don't know why.

The sheets warm against my body, going from cool to lukewarm to toasty as my thumb toys with the button. My heart beats too fast, though that's probably the caffeine. Shit. I'm trying to keep a positive attitude about all of this, but I'm pretty wired. This little box better pack some big time sleep magic or this isn't going to work.

To Glenn's credit, we did achieve total blackness in here. I pressed a rolled up towel along the crack at the bottom of the door as per his instructions, and that blocked out the last sliver of light from the hall. So that part, at least, works in my favor.

Maybe I need to get comfortable. Maybe that's the cause for hesitation.

I adjust in the bed, pulling the blanket down off of my shoulders so it only comes up to my sternum or so. Then I fix the sheet so it's still covering up to my neck. I wiggle my shoulder blades a little as though it might help me feel more settled in. When that doesn't change anything, I kick my feet a few times, like maybe I can work some of the restlessness out of my system that way. Kicking makes my legs feel warm, and the tingle of static electricity grips every leg hair and pulls it toward the sheet. That combination of warm and tingling is kind of pleasant somehow.

No excuses left, I depress the button.

The blue LED bulb lights up, vanquishing the dark. Blue light reflects off of the walls and reminds me that there are blankets duct taped over the windows, which I guess I already sort of forgot about in the dark.

I set the box on the nightstand, so the light will shine onto the ceiling above me. I lie back, already oddly conscious of my breathing patterns. After a few seconds, the blue pulsing begins. The light dims slowly down to nothing and brightens. Something about it does seem just like eyelids drooping closed, though mine are open. I adjust my breathing to match its rhythm – in as the light swells to full brightness, out as it fades to black.

So here I am, awake in the dark once more, doing weird breathing exercises. In retrospect, I'm really glad Glenn isn't in here breathing up the place from the comfort of his la-z-boy. It'd be too weird.

I focus on my breathing. The light shines and recedes and shines and recedes. A peace comes over me, a stillness. Just as my mind clears of all other thoughts but the light and the breathing, a rapid fire montage of Louise plays in my head – she hugs me in the doorway, she laughs with her mouth full of milkshake, she walks down the hall with no pants on, she smiles in the moonlight in the backseat of the Explorer - and I'm alert again.

Wide awake in the dark. My mind scatters like it often does, one memory leading to another and another. I sigh, and that knocks my breathing out of rhythm.

Damn it.

I blink a few times and stare into the blue light on the ceiling. I can't let frustration or anxiety derail this. Too much depends on our success. I focus again on my respiration. Slow inhale. Slow exhale.

I lie still and think of nothing. Time passes. I'm not sure how much. The machine has options for a 7 minute cycle or a 25 minute cycle. I went for the longer one, so I know it's been less than 25 minutes, I guess.

I am just vaguely aware of the heat crawling into my face, that sleepy anesthetic warmth that comes over you in slumber, but I don't let my mind dwell on the sensation.

I watch the blue illumination extinguished repeatedly. It is the only thing. I almost feel like I'm not even physically here. I am like part of the light.

I feel my eyelids sag a little, and I almost jerk to alertness to wake myself up out of habit, like when you realize that you're falling asleep in class, but I don't do it. I stay zoned out, somehow not all the way conscious of my physical being. My eyes drift into a half closed position, but it feels far away.

I let myself forget about them. I let my body go a little more, and it's like my consciousness moves out into the ever slowing pulse of light. It hovers there, a couple of feet above my chest.

I am weightless. I am all energy, only energy. And the things that have worried me and hurt me suddenly don't seem to matter, the things of the Earth suddenly seem insignificant. It's all so small. The meaning we put into Earthly things, be they objects or even flesh itself - it isn't real. It's all in our heads.

Energy.

Energy is all that is real.

I think of Earthly goods – sports cars and big screen TVs and ipads and such – and as they flash through my consciousness, I can feel them try to pull me back down, but they can't. They can't stick in my mind. I float on, and they all fall away.

And the light fades out and does not return, and I am in the black stillness, and all is quiet. I am calm. It feels like something is missing, something important, but I am not alarmed.

I move forward into the blackness. I lean into it and direct myself that way. It almost feels like something pulls me, but I think it's more like the energy flows the way I want.

I make steady progress for what feels like a long time. I wouldn't call the pace slow, but it's relaxed. I guess when you're moving in darkness, it's harder to gauge the speed anyway. It's more like just the sense of motion.

It gets weird, after a while, to just drift in empty space like this. I keep my calm, but there's an uneasiness out on the edge of things trying to creep into my energy. Maybe it's a coldness.

I stop.

A light. A tiny pin prick of light emerges before me, a dot of bluish white illumination disrupting the black nothing all around. It looks to be far, far in the distance. And somehow it is a relief to see it, though I didn't feel anxious before. I am happy to look upon it. I guess I like lights.

I walk toward it.

Huh?

Yes. I am not directing energy anymore, not flowing. I am walking now. In the dark, I can't see my feet kicking forward one after the other to take steps, but I can feel it.

If I'm walking, there must be something under my feet, too. It all feels a little far away, a little numb like I'm asleep, but I think I'm barefoot. And the floor feels smooth and cool, like painted concrete in a basement or garage.

I take a deep breath, and the air feels cool in my throat. Ah. I'm breathing now, too. I can't remember if I was before. I think not, but maybe I just wasn't conscious of it.

I walk toward the light for a long while, inching ever closer to the end of this black tunnel.

Wait.

How did I get here? How did I make my way to this tunnel? I try to think back. It feels like I can almost remember it somehow, but I can't. The best I can conjure is a flash and dim of blue light. It's not much to go on.

This lack of memory doesn't concern me greatly, though. It's a familiar feeling, to not remember how I arrived at a location. I think I probably have experienced this before.

I walk and walk, and the dot of light grows. It's hard to believe that it's not a ping-pong-ball-sized source of illumination as it appears. It's the hole far at the end of this dark tunnel. At least, that's what I think.

Now, it's not expanding to fill the horizon as quickly as I'd like, but it is getting bigger. I'm not complaining. Don't look a gift hole in the hole and what not.

As I walk, I feel the cold creep into my feet. They seem to be getting more sensitive. I can't say the same for the rest of me, but my feet feel more awake.

The scuff and patter of my footsteps echoes all around me, and for the first time it occurs to me how massive this tunnel is. I sense by the reverberations that the walls are nowhere near me. They exist somewhere out in this expanse of darkness. I think just the idea of this helps that chill begin to spread from my feet to the rest of me.

And I wonder, were the sounds of my footsteps always there? Or did they just fade in now?

I can't say for sure.

But I don't let any kind of anxiety take root in my head; an unease maybe, but nothing approaching panic.

I walk. I focus on the movement, on the new depths of sensation traveling up and down my calves like surging currents of electricity. The muscle balls and releases with each step. I can't see it, so I picture the muscle flexing.

And as I key in on my lower legs, it occurs to me that I can feel fabric tug against my knees as they bend. I'm not nude.

So that's good.

I guess I was a little worried about getting out into the light to find my scrotum staring back at me. Instead I look forward to seeing some relaxed fit denim by the feel of it. Would be weird if I was wearing sweatpants or something, right?

OK, wait again.

What am I doing? Do I have an objective here?

I can't think of one. Did I forget it? Did I ever have one?

My mind goes blank as I reach out for these memories, and the sound of my feet padding over the concrete comes back to the forefront of my consciousness.

The dark tunnel stretches on and on. The light looks to be just bigger than a baseball now. It seems to be growing faster, whether that makes any sense or not.

My fingers feel the cold now, the chill spreading from the tips down to the place where knuckle meets palm. It stings. I rub my hands together, but it's sort of like rubbing frozen fish sticks against each other and hoping they'll thaw.

"Friction cannot help you here," a voice says, and I jump, startled.

The surge of adrenalin that shoots up and down my limbs feels colder still. My torso jerks. My hands squeeze into fists.

After a second I realize it was my voice.

I am dumb.

In retrospect, the words seemed to come from outside of me somehow, though, and that seems familiar, too. Yeah. Yeah, I have heard a voice before in a situation like this, haven't I? A girl's voice, I think.

Think, Grobnagger, think.

Amity.

Yes!

Her I remember.

I see her in my head. I see her in the photo album at Glenn's, sad in every shot. I see her running away from me over the dunes, my johnson swaying back and forth like an elephant's trunk. I even see her meditating in a cornfield, though I wasn't there to witness that firsthand. That image is encoded in my brain the way I imagined it, I guess. It pops up like a dream just like the others.

She is interesting to me. Sometimes I think she might be like me. Is that why I remember her? Hard to say, but it brings back a lot.

We're going to the other world to help her. That's my

objective. I need to find Amity. This tunnel must be the way, right?

And then I remember covering the windows with blankets and the blue light and the coffee and all of it. It all makes sense. I think knowing what the hell is going on helps me walk a little faster, so that's good.

CHAPTER 16

By the time I near the mouth of the tunnel, I realize how huge it is. I feel tiny, like an ant walking through the Grand Canyon.

Shit. I probably should've compared it to a really huge mouth instead since I called it the mouth of the tunnel. Like an ant walking out of a whale's mouth or something like that. Too late. I totally blew it. I'm sorry.

In some detail I can see the forest on the other side of this threshold. The green of the leaves stands out against the gray of the sky. Somehow it's not real yet, though. It won't be real until the light touches my skin, I think.

I can see my arms and feet in the shade now, at least, and if I strain I can make out my legs, though they look darker as they're clad in jeans. It's good to see these limbs again, like being united with old friends. Plus, I'm wearing pants this time. Bonus.

I hear something squeak and crackle out, and it occurs to me that the sound isn't echoing around in the tunnel at all. Not sure what that means. I think about stopping to listen for whatever it was to make more noise, but at this point I want to get out of this place as soon as possible. I press forward.

The cold has a pretty good hold on me now, from head to feet. My fingers and toes ache with that painful level of chilliness. I want to run the last few hundred yards out of here, but it would hurt my feet too much. I walk, as ever, but I picture myself cutting open a small animal and warming my hands and feet in there. I mean, I wouldn't actually mutilate an animal like that, but damn would it feel good, right?

I squint as the light gets brighter and brighter. Even with all of this time to adjust, my pupils seem unable to cope with the changes. I rub at my eyes, and it feels so good, like I can erase all of the sleep and tired and the sting of the light if I just keep pressing my fingers on them, so I do that.

The sound around me changes – it kind of opens up - and when I pull my hands away from my face, I'm outside of the tunnel. I look back at the hole I've just walked out of and find it carved into red rock that seems to go straight up as far as I can see.

The forested terrain out here doesn't look right to be situated so close to a mountain – it's too vibrant and green to be growing out of rock, you know? And the cliff wall itself is somehow too uniform in its 90 degree angle of ascent. It doesn't necessarily look man made. Crevices and serrated edges and other imperfections etch their lines into the stone. Still, something is off about it.

I scratch the back of my neck and move on. I make it about six paces farther when her voice intervenes.

"Are you there?"

I stop.

"Yeah," I say.

"Good," she says. "You don't have to talk out loud, though. We are connected for now. "

"Oh," I say out loud.

Damn. I always get real smooth as soon as I'm talking to a

girl.

"Oh," I say again in my head.

She laughs. Her laugh consists of a rapid series of inhaled breaths, that repetition of squeaks as the air rushes in. It reminds me of the laugh of a nerdy girl in a sitcom. Maybe a little cuter, though.

"I brought you here," she says. "That's why we're connected. I'm glad you can understand me this time."

"Yeah," I say. "Well, we drank a shitload of coffee to try to keep our minds sharp. Seems like it worked. Did you bring Glenn, too?"

"I'm working on it. He might not be deep enough asleep yet. I think it happens between sleep cycles. If I'm calling on you right as you shift into the deepest sleep, the connection opens up. I'm not certain, though."

"Where are you?"

"I'll tell you, but I don't think it'll be of much use: I'm in the woods. You?"

"Woods. Just walked out of a big ass tunnel."

"I see."

"So is there some way I can find you? Some set of landmarks or something?"

"Mm... Not really. Bunch of trees, mainly. Branches. Leaves. Stuff like that."

"Damn it," I say. I think about this a moment. "You ever see a huge red cliff type deal? Real gargantuan cave leading into it?"

"Not that I recall," she says.

"Yeah, you'd probably remember this thing," I say, pointing at the cliff wall even though I know she can't see my gesture.

"Real big cave."

I feel weird hanging out by the cave, so I start picking my way through the foliage as I think to her. It sounds like she yawns before she goes on.

"It gets weird out here. Things have a way of changing on you. I can't decide if the landscape itself changes, or if something out here wears holes into your memory so it only feels like everything around you morphs and melts into new shapes that surprise you because you don't remember them. Either way, though, that's how it feels: perpetual surprise and confusion, like living in a dream."

"Yeah, I see what you mean," I say.

My strides chop and stutter in dinky little steps, all careful as hell. I guess I'm scared of stepping on something weird with bare feet. The ground feels cool and soft underfoot for the most part. Out here I'm walking on a layer of mulch comprised mostly of dead leaves.

"So hey, are you in trouble or something?" I say.

"What?" she says. "No. I'm just sitting in the woods."

"Oh," I say. "Well, we thought you might be in trouble or something. I mean, I guess we thought that's why you were trying to contact us."

I bend at the waist to pass under a crisscross of low hanging branches. Leaves tickle all of the places where my skin is exposed.

"No," she says, and I think I hear the faintest edge of incredulity creep into her voice. "You two are the ones that are in trouble."

I stop in my tracks, still folded in half with leaves brushing at the back of my neck.

100

"How do you mean?" I say.

"Farber," she says. "He walks among us, Grobnagger. I've seen him out here, though only from a distance. He means you harm."

"Harm?" I say. "How do you know that if you've only seen him from a distance?"

She is quiet.

I shuffle forward to a place where I can stand up and stretch out my back and neck. The trees grow a little sparser here, a thick tangle of brush taking their place.

"I can't remember how I know," she says. "But I know that I know. Does that make sense?"

"Yeah," I say. "I know exactly what you mean."

CHAPTER 17

This brain to brain conversation feels so much like being on the phone. I keep wanting to put my hand by my ear out of habit. Instead I trudge deeper into the brush, green coming up to my knees. My feet pad on firmer soil now, though I'm tramping down a layer of various grasses as well.

"So why are you doing this?" I say.

"Doing what?" she says.

"Why are you staying out here?" I say. "Why don't you want to come back to the real world or whatever?"

She clucks her tongue against the roof of her mouth a few times like she's doing some kind of mental math. When I remember that she is doing this in her head rather than out loud, it seems funny somehow.

"I don't know," she says.

That's it. She doesn't go on. The silence hangs in the air a moment, but then some grass swishes against my pant legs as I step through a particularly thick patch.

"You don't know?" I say. "What the hell kind of an answer is that?"

She makes a throaty noise that reminds me of an elf dying in a role playing game.

"It's boring there," she says. "I mean, sure, there are potentially interesting things there, but I mostly understand the way things work pretty well. I can see the range of possibilities in the paths before me there. Out here, anything is possible. I don't understand it much at all, and it's great."

"So you like it because you don't understand it?" I say. "You might be even weirder than I thought."

"When you think about it," she says. "Aren't the possibilities in life always better than the realities? When you dream of how things might be, that's when you're at your happiest. That's when you're most excited, most captivated. Once your dream becomes a reality, even if things go as well as you could possibly hope, it can never quite live up to the excitement in that original possibility, can it? Nothing can ever fill us up the way we think it might, can it?"

I let my fingers stroke the divots and craters pocking the tree bark as I pass an oak.

"I don't know," I say. "I guess not."

"Not much to say now, eh? You must know I'm right," she says. "Based on what I've heard about you, this is probably all stuff you already know. I mean, you're not exactly an outgoing guy with a can do spirit, right? Don't you not have any friends or family?"

I kind of wonder what all she's heard about me, but I push the conversation in a different direction.

"You do, though. So what about your family?" I say. "I mean, your Dad worries about you. I'm sure your Mom does, too. Do you feel bad about that? And don't you get lonely out here, anyhow? Don't you miss people?"

Her imaginary tongue clucks again but just once this time.

"Way I see it, we all walk our own paths based on what we think is right," she says. "I can't fix things for other people. I

103

can't be responsible for that. I have to do my own thing, because this is the only chance I have to do it. There's no do over for good behavior if you waste your life trying to please other people. You don't get another crack at it for being a good Samaritan. Every second you waste is gone forever. You never get it back."

I crunch through some dried-out stalks that look like a cross between corn and cat tails.

"So you don't feel guilty. I can understand that, but you have to get lonely sometimes, right?" I say.

"Fuck that," she says. "To me, lonely is being surrounded by people and never feeling connected to any of them. Staying there, fighting in vain against that inevitability would be a lifetime of loneliness. Maybe my way will, too, but I'm doing what makes sense to me. I'm trying."

The tinge of anger in her voice surprises me, but I can't disagree with her, at least not enough to argue. She goes on:

"Maybe what happens out here is just as pointless as what happens there, but I feel like if I buy into the emptiness all around me there – the worship of technology and pharmaceuticals and sports and sit-coms playing in HD on big screen TVs – I feel like if I accept that materialistic worldview as the order of the universe, I am putting my faith in nothing. Out here, maybe I don't exactly know what I'm putting my faith into, but it's something or at least it might be. I'd rather put my faith in something, you know? Something is better than nothing. Anything is."

As she talks, my feet plant themselves in the ground. I move no longer. I stand and listen. When she seems finished, I remain motionless. The air feels so still just now.

"Don't you think it's just energy, though?" I say. "See, Glenn thinks it's energy that connects us all. It kind of reflects pieces of all of us and in that way seems to have a personality, but in the end it's just energy."

"It could be," she says. "There's no easy answer here. Even if it's something like that, though, isn't that more worthy of exploring than the material world?"

I look up at the sky, the billowing blanket of gray and white fluff above me.

"Maybe," I say.

"Don't you get the feeling this place likes you?" she says. "And I mean you personally, Grobnagger. Seems to me it likes you in particular."

"Is that why it had the hooded man... Is that why it had you strangle me over and over?" I say.

She laughs.

"It was trying to teach you something," she says. "That's what I think. "

After a pause she continues:

"I didn't know what was going on during that, by the way," she says. "I just had the overwhelming urge to, you know, kill you."

"Yeah, it seems like I inspire that a lot in people these days," I say. "They mean me harm and all."

She laughs again, harder this time. It kind of sounds like a seal's bark, but an especially cute seal, I'd say. Not one of the ones with the tusks and the crazy mustaches or whatever. Are those walruses?

Wait. What's a sea lion? It could be either a walrus or a sea lion I'm thinking of, but yeah. You know what? I'm going to go ahead and say she doesn't sound like either one. So there.

A real cute seal is what I'm getting at here.

"What?" she says.

Fuck. Did I think that out loud to her?

She laughs harder still, so I guess I did. I try not to picture baby seals clapping for fish at Sea World. I don't know if I can transmit pictures to her or just dialog, but I would rather not risk it.

CHAPTER 18

I've been trying to walk in more or less a straight line, but I frequently have to go off course to get around various barriers. Just now it's a giant patch of thorny looking bushes.

"So what's with all these tricks you guys have figured out?" I say. "I can't do any cool shit."

"Like what tricks?" she says.

"Well, you figured out how to pull me here and talk to me through your mind, right?" I say. "And your Dad healed himself and cut a doorway to this place. I want to do kick ass stuff like that."

"I can show you one right now. An easy one," she says. "Lie down."

I look down at the ground. The sand and scraggly weeds don't look that inviting.

"Well, what is it?" I say. "I should know what I'm getting into before I commit to it."

"Just lie down on your back if you want to learn something," she says. "It's interesting. I promise."

I ease myself down to a seated position and lie back. Plants tickle my neck. The sand grits itself into the backs of my arms, and the heat works its way through my t-shirt to press its warmth into the flesh on my back.

"All right. I'm down," I say. "Now what?"

"OK. Close your eyes and feel your consciousness rising up through your eyebrows," she says. "Don't think about it too hard. Just let it happen. Feel it happening."

I try this. The muscles in my forehead contort a few different directions. I open my eyelids a slit to confirm that nothing awesome is transpiring.

"I don't think anything happened," I say. "Actually, I think I just raised my eyebrows, so I probably look pretty surprised, at least."

She laughs.

"No, not toward the top of your head," she says. "Toward the sky. Feel it flowing like water from just above that spot where your nose meets your forehead. Feel yourself disconnect."

I try to let myself feel these things she says. I imagine the sensation of the place where my thoughts transpire ascending through a spot in the center of my skull. I feel it trickle upward, squeezed a bit to fit through the skull spot and then expanding once it's free, floating more than flowing now, drifting up like a buoy popping up from below the surface and bobbing about, turning over a few times. But it all feels far away, too. A passing feeling that is forgotten as soon as you're done experiencing it.

"Did it work?" she says.

I peel open my eyes to find myself floating just above the tree line. It feels like a dream. And then I rotate, and I see myself – my body, I guess – lying on the sandy patch below. I floated out of myself.

This scares me. From this height, all I can think about is falling, so I float back down some. It's a slow process.

"Hello? Did it work?" she says.

Oh. I forgot to answer.

"Yeah," I say, looking down on my body. I look peaceful enough. "Am I going to be able to... like, get back in there?"

She laughs again, the rapid gasping inhalations.

"Of course. You'll be fine," she says. "Pretty cool, though, right?"

"Yeah," I say. "Just... I'm going to get back in there."

I push myself back into that place just above the spot between my eyes. All goes dark, and I feel constricted for a second. Then I open my eyes. I am myself again.

"You're a bit of a nervous pervis aren't you?" she says.

"What?" I say. "No. I mean, I just wanted to make sure."

"It's OK," she says. "I just thought you'd be more excited to try it out."

I pat at the ground, the dirt coarse against my fingertips. Satisfied that the land remains solid, I stand and dust myself off.

"So hey," I say. "Why do you think that's possible? I mean, my real body is back in bed asleep, right? I'm already disconnected from it. Why would I do that again here? It's like a dream within a dream or something."

"Well, I'm not 100% sure, but I think of it like this: We have avatars on this plane that look like our physical selves because it's what we understand. It makes us comfortable," she says. "But we can sort of disconnect from it into pure energy."

I scrape my toe into the ground.

"That makes sense," I say.

I trek over a patch of barren earth, sandy soil slithering up between my toes. The dirt is the exact shade of the coat of a

Prussian blue cat, gray with just the faintest blue tint.

"So what do you even do out here?" I say. "Apart from no one to talk to, there's no TV to watch, no internet, nothing to read."

"Aw, don't worry about me. There's a lot of terrain to wander over. A lot of thoughts to think. I manage to make my own fun," she says.

"What does that entail, though?" I say. "From a practical standpoint, I mean."

"A little bit of everything, I guess," she says. "When you read or watch TV, what are you really doing? You're triggering things in your imagination, right? It's not the words on the page that entertain you or teach you or change you, it's what they evoke in your imagination. Would you agree with that?"

"Yeah, I guess so," I say.

"Well, out here your imagination gets going on its own," she says. "You don't need external stimulus to elicit the good stuff. It just pours out pictures and ideas day and night, and you realize that your imagination is a world within a world, maybe even a universe within a universe, yeah? Who needs the outside world when you came equipped with your own? You've got your own universe sitting idle in your brain pan. I mean, if you bother learning how to use it, anyhow."

I find a spot where the ground is warm and stop and wiggle my toes in the sand. I don't really know what to say, but I talk anyway.

"I don't know. It doesn't seem right somehow," I say.

"What doesn't?" she says.

"Spending a lifetime alone voluntarily," I say, and the irony of my words isn't lost on me, considering my prior position on the matter. "It seems like an empty existence to me."

She is quiet for a time. I don't know why this particular spot in the sand is so warm, but patches of skin on my feet now feel on the verge of blistering, in a good way if that makes sense. Like right now, it feels good like a hot bath at the perfect temp, but if it were 5 degrees hotter, my flesh would be crisping up like fried chicken.

I'm almost ready to check if she's still there, but she answers me.

"Where do you think philosophers look for answers?" she says. "Sure, they're educated, well read, all of that. But when they go to create or lay down some new tract, they sit down by themselves and write, don't they? They look inside. Not outside. I'm not a philosopher, but that's what it's about for me. Don't confuse it. It's not about loneliness for the sake of loneliness at all. I mean, I brought you here, didn't I?"

"Well, yeah," I say.

"And we're talking now, and I'm enjoying it," she says. "I'm not here to be alone. I'm here to look inside. It just so happens that I'm probably going to spend a lot of this time alone in the process, and I'm OK with that."

That makes sense in a way. I go to tell her so, but my words catch in my throat and come out wrong:

"I'm some, I'm some, I'm some, I'm some kind, I'm some kind, I'm some kind of, I'm some kind of a, I'm some kind of a memory."

I don't know what I'm saying. These don't seem like the words I meant to speak, but I can't remember for sure. I feel like I'm falling.

"A memory, a memory, a memory."

I finally stop talking. I can feel the heat in my face, can just make out my cheeks going red at the edge of my vision, and I'm embarrassed. Something crazy is happening to me, I can't talk or move or breathe, I'm fucking dying for all I know, and even still I'm really embarrassed. That's the overwhelming emotional response here. I feel dumb.

"Ah. I hope I talk to you again soon," she says.

She doesn't seem alarmed, but I don't know how she might be experiencing this. To her it's just some gibberish, I guess.

I collapse on the line where the sand ends, my torso sprawling among thigh high grass while my feet and legs still touch the warm of the sand. Spindles of plant life whisk stems and stalks across my face as I descend. The icy green fingers plead with my face to cool down, but it's no use. The heat just bloats in my cheeks and swells further.

Air bursts from my lungs in fits both choppy and involuntary. My throat chokes out nonsense words like, "Snarf!" over and over. I sound like a Miniature Pinscher coughing up chunks of rawhide.

And the light seems to dim about me. And I gag and hack and wriggle the best I can, arms knocking over grass, toenails scraping in the sand, though my motor skills seem inarticulate. And my neck arches back to look at the gray sky going darker still. And my shoulders shimmy without my telling them to, like a weird palsy vibrating my upper body.

It's no use, I know now.

So I try to be calm. And I try to be still. And I try to wait for the black to overtake me.

Darkness surrounds me. Warmth envelops me. I bring a hand

to my face. My fingers feel a little rough. The flesh along my jaw and cheek bones is toasty, oddly slack somehow, a little numb. It's not unpleasant. This verifies my suspicion. The other world, the grass, that surge of fever heat invading my face – they're all gone.

This new warmth strikes me as familiar, though. I go to sit up, but something prevents my knees from bending all the way. Huh? My hands pat around. Fabric pulls taut over my body. I know this, don't I? Oh yeah. A blanket.

That triggers it. The memories wash back over me, and the corresponding images flicker through my frontal lobe: Two pots of coffee, multiple layers of duct tape stretched over the edges of bedspreads to block out the windows, the little black box shining its blue light onto the ceiling.

My sense of my setting restored, I lie back, my head sinking into the pillow. A deep breath expands my rib cage, and it shrinks back to normal as the wind escapes me all slow.

I open my eyes and look into the blackness, blink a few times, see nothing.

Now that I'm over freaking out about a blanket pinning my legs down, the relief fades away and a sense of excitement tinged with melancholy settles over me.

I remember all of the things that Amity said. Sure, she said Farber meant me harm, but I kind of figured that for a strong possibility already. It was all the things she said about looking inside that I can't stop thinking about.

On one hand, I find great excitement in talking to someone so full of passion for things close to my own heart. On the other, her outlook has such a fatalism to it, it just makes me sad. I think she is wrong about being alone, just as I was wrong about being alone. I don't think pushing everyone away is a path to any kind of happiness, not anymore.

Life is like a choose your own adventure book, and she keeps taking the gloomiest route. But if you choose gloom, you get gloom. That's how it goes.

Like me? I sometimes think I just preferred being sad in a way. I constructed a narrative to make it make sense. I held my head sideways to see my life as I wanted to see it, to see a black and white explanation for how I felt as though it's an unchangeable thing. But we're all responsible for how we feel, too, at least in part.

I am not perfect, but I can try. I can try to do better. I can try to be happy. There's nothing wrong with that.

And just as these words cross through my head, I hear the floorboards squeak on the other side of the room.

My respiration cuts off mid breath. My diaphragm clenches, and my ribcage quakes.

Someone is in the room with me.

CHAPTER 19

Adrenalin gushes into my head, and I feel the pangs of chemical excitement race up and down my frame. The dark around me seems much darker all of the sudden.

I don't breathe. I don't move.

I listen.

I hear nothing.

Based on the total lack of light, I know that the bedroom door remains shut with the rolled up towel still blocking out the crack at the bottom. Did someone come in here, close the door and put the towel back? And if so, what for? And also why did they just wait in the dark for however long I've been lying here thinking?

What a creep.

My brain races through the possibilities. None of them make much sense. I know a cat wasn't in here when I closed the room up. I know there's no reason for Glenn to do this. Could it be the night stalker? I'm not even sure it's the night, actually, but could it be a home invasion?

I sit up with care, making sure to remain soundless. I keep my legs straight out, too scared the friction of leg moving against sheet will be audible. I gaze into the abyss in front of me as though I'll suddenly be able to see in the dark now that I'm upright.

I try to stop myself from thinking it, but it's too late. A replay of Amity's voice plays in my head, emphasizing that Farber walks among us, that he means us harm.

Is that possible? Could he be here now?

Could this be why Glenn never arrived in the other world as planned?

Considering that prospect leads to more adrenalin. The electrical chill surges all through me again. Sweat oozes out of my forehead and slicks up the back of my neck. For a second I picture the beads of perspiration there, my neck skin rippling with goosebumps as the cold feeling comes over me once more.

I scoot the blanket off of my legs a few inches and wait. Then I slide it down a little more. Wait. All holds still and black and silent around me.

With two more bedspread scoots, my legs are free. I'm hesitant to actually move them, though. Can't make a sound now.

My breath goes shallow, quiet. The air enters and retreats almost at the same time, scraping back and forth over the dried-out pink flesh of my throat. I try to not focus on it. I try to think of anything but my respiration as I'm worried about psyching myself out and hyperventilating. Frozen here in this seated position, though, I have nothing else to think about.

What if I just imagined the sound? It's not impossible. I don't think I would've panicked like this, though. My right brain, my animal instincts would know the difference. Some creeping little doubt would have prevented me from freaking out all the way.

The floorboard moans again, a mournful, high pitched creak that sounds like it should have a question mark at the end of it.

Well, shit.

The ensuing panic spurs me to action. Moving like a silent movie, I bring my knees up and crab walk toward the side of the bed that seems to be the opposite of where the sound came from. My hands reach off the bed, down into black nothing. The floor seems a long way off, farther down than it has any right to be, but I find it.

I ease myself onto the floor back first like that - my hands plant on the cool of the hardwood, walk my torso out a little, and then my legs swing down after. All motion remains controlled, careful, silent, bordering on slow motion. I almost feel like a gymnast doing some awful moves on that horse thing or something. A terrible, terrible bedroom gymnast.

I hover there, ass suspended a few inches off of the floor, legs sticking straight out, all of my body weight on my hands. I listen. Nothing. Even so, I freeze. I wait.

In time, my wrists sting, and my forearms quiver a tad.

After what seems like a few minutes, I release my body weight, letting myself rest on the floor butt first, then feet. After another moment spent motionless, I lean forward so my face almost touches my knees. I want to be sure my ears stay above the bed line, so no sounds are muffled.

Something moves. Fabric, I think. I listen again.

There's a scuffing noise, and the floor croaks, a deeper sound this time. A second later it squeaks again, another question. I feel the wood planks vibrate and sag ever so faintly beneath my palms as the weight on the floor shifts. Definitely footsteps. The sounds seem to be getting closer to the bed but approaching from the other side of where I'm seated.

117

I sprawl into push-up position and crawl forward, rounding the corner of the bed. I don't know. I guess my instinct is to go right at this guy but from an angle that will surprise him. I'm flanking him. Or her. Probably him.

I remember reading that you're statistically better off to be the aggressor if someone breaks into your house. That I shall do. Be it the night stalker, Farber or whomever, he must go down, and he must go down hard.

I move like a sloth, poking one arm out, waiting, bringing a leg forward, waiting. I hesitate at the bottom of the bed, hugging against the foot of the mattress to avoid getting stepped on or kicked. I want to get a better idea of exactly where he stands before I go around the next corner. Believe me, the last thing I want to do is crawl right into him.

That would make a funny story some day, I guess, if I did crawl into him. For him, I mean. He'd have a hilarious burglary story about the time the guy crawled right into his legs, and he snapped the poor bastard's neck before he could even get to his feet.

I listen to the silence, the blank nothing emptiness. My ears try to hear something in it. My eyes try to see something in it.

I wait and sweat and wait and sweat some more. Perspiration battles the heat crawling from my torso up onto my face, but it's no use. I'm all warm. I bet rosy patches blotch my cheeks.

He clears his throat. It's not a full on throat clear but more of a faint throat noise. A grumble of mucus and soft flesh.

So it's real. This is really happening. A person violates this room. They invade. They infest. They trespass. A real live human being stands less than 10 feet from where I crouch. And based on the deep bass of the grunt, that human being is an adult male.

I snake forward into the open, leaving the safety of my spot right along the bed. I now have a good feel for where this guy idles.

And I mean him harm.

CHAPTER 20

The room wears its darkness like a black blanket. I can't see anything. It muffles the sound, too, so I can't hear anything, either.

Not the best of conditions in terms of picking a moment to run full speed at someone, but you work with what you have.

I square my shoulders toward where I'm pretty sure he is standing. Still crouching, I get on my feet. My arms lift at my sides and go into a wide curl, as though I'm about to hug him.

I'm not.

This arm move is premature in any case, I know. More of precaution than a preparation. It goes hit then wrap, not the the other way around. I'll be too busy torpedoing my shoulders at him to have my arms preemptively in hug position.

My heart beats so hard that my ribcage convulses in rhythm. Feels like an alien wants to spurt out of my chest cavity. I wouldn't even mind that if the critter would help me fight this guy.

I angle my torso forward to get more of my weight in front of my feet so I can push off better, winding up in a position a couple of notches shy of a sprinter's stance. Acceleration will be key, and there's not much room to get going in here.

So much adrenalin now that my arms tremor and the rest of me spasms off and on. My thoughts flutter. Nausea throbs in my gut.

This is it.

Life or death in 3.

2.

1.

I blitz him, rushing forward at top speed, though the world plays in slow motion in my head. My feet churn in perfect unison, pushing off and sliding forth. I get off and going with a nice burst.

A few paces later, I hurl myself at what I deem the proper spot. My body goes horizontal. My arms go wide.

I collide with him. This is good. But it's a glancing blow. My right shoulder slides off what I think is his chest, only managing to knock him back a half of a step or so.

My arms grapple at him like spider legs, and I hook him pretty good. As my momentum carries me forward rapidly, I get my feet back under me just in time to use it to catapult him into the wall even harder than I hit it.

The bang of my shoulder hitting drywall is loud, but his wall slam sounds much more violent. I can hear the hole being ripped into Glenn's wall, hopefully with this guy's face.

It sounds like multiple concussions.

I go to stand, but our limbs are tangled. It takes a moment of scrambling and grabbing to figure out what is what. We squirm in the dark. I wind up partially upright, leaning on one knee. My fingers graze over emaciated cheek bones and eyelids and grip on the stubble on the shaved head, all prickly like the sharp side of Velcro. And the details of the cranium against my hands confirms what I knew deep down all along.

It's Farber. I don't know how, but it's him.

He wriggles his head free from my grip, and my claws scrabble until they find purchase on his torso. I feel ribs through his shirt, and when I make contact with his skin, he's all sinewy and clammy and weird to the touch. I can't help but picture his flesh all slimy like those two little tentacle antennas protruding from a slug's head.

I lose my balance, tumbling, crashing onto the floor, but I keep my grip and pull him down with me.

Rising to my knees, I jerk him up by the torso and slam him back down. Hard. He's so gaunt. It's more like tossing around a slimy mannequin than a man.

He gasps for breath, his throat struggling for wind, the sounds coming out of him all shrill and dry like a dying bird. I think maybe I knocked the wind out of him.

Either way, the noises are like a bullseye for my fists. I descend on him, straddling his rib cage and letting endless punches rain down.

I pummel his stupid face in.

The heat creeps all the way into my head now. A fevered glow radiates from my face, and I don't hear anything anymore. I break open his face so the red pours out. I don't see it. I feel it. I feel my fists pounding flesh against bone like two meat tenderizers flattening a steak. I feel the cartilage in his nose break into smaller and smaller pieces. I feel the warm blood pour from my knuckles. I see the black around me take on a red tint.

And when the light cuts a wedge-shaped swath of gray into the darkness, it almost doesn't register at first. I keep punching, keep feeling the fire burning in my head like nothing else is real, but part of me gets that feeling like I'm about to realize something important.

"Grobnagger," a voice behind me says.

My fists slow and then stop. It's a weird feeling. It's like I had committed to punching this face forever, backing out now feels like a loss.

"Stand up, son," the voice says. "Are you all right?"

I don't say anything. I look at the face, but it still lies shrouded in darkness. All I can make out is wetness moving in the black.

I stand, consenting finally to the demand made of me.

I turn to see Glenn flipping the light switch a few times. It doesn't work.

"What..." he says. "What happened in here?"

I still don't say anything, so he steps into the room to get a better look at the body.

"Holy shit," he says.

His voice trembles a little. It's the first time I've heard Glenn sound this scared, but there's nothing to be scared of. I handled it. I follow the path of his eyes to the figure on the floor.

The triangle of light leaning through the doorway paints a picture in the muted tones of half light. Farber's legs sprawl into the path of what's visible, black dickies leading down to boots with a waffle pattern on the bottoms. His black shirted torso stretches into the darkness, the details of his face obscured by the shadows.

I stride over to the body and look down on it, my feet almost touching the leg. I consider giving a little kick as a test, but I decide not to. I don't think there's much of a point.

"Is he..." Glenn says. "Is he dead?"

I say nothing. My mouth hangs open, panting like a dog's. I realize this has been the case for a long while now.

And then a sound creaks out of the dead man, out of his mouth. At first I think this is some kind of death rattle or post death nervous twitch.

No.

He's laughing.

Glenn backpedals a few paces to the doorway.

I don't know if it's Glenn's cowardice that triggers it, but the next thing I know, I'm back on the body. My knees pin his arms to the ground. My hands close around the throat.

"Oh, no!" Farber says in a mock tone, still chuckling. "Don't do that. You'll smother me!"

I squeeze. I crush. I clamp his throat closed for good.

His clammy skin seems to go firm now. The scrawny physique goes rigid, suddenly seeming more lean and hard and wiry than floppy and weak. He bucks a few times. It's not enough to free his arms, but he keeps me from securing my grip fully.

He also shifts us enough to shake his face out into the gray light. I see the destruction I've done, the smashed parts, and purpled bits, and his red insides, the wet life juice spilling out into the world. But I can still tell it's him. Even through all of the swelling and bruising, I can see it.

The struggle goes on for what must be a few seconds but seems like a long time, and my sense of control over the situation only grows. His torso quakes. His hips twist. I'm too strong for him, and he knows it. He keeps fighting, but I can feel the defeat in him. His moves don't have the same life in them. His flesh seems to sag once more. He's just going through the motions now. It's a matter of time.

My hands press and flex and squash his neck down to nothing.

I see a jerky motion out of the corner of my eye, and I look up in time to see Glenn's hand cup his mouth, trying to hold back vomit and failing. A gush of brown sprays between his fingers, opaque and lumpy. He buckles at the waist, letting the barf slap on the wood floor and spatter against the wall.

We make eye contact as he heaves again. I see shame in Glenn's expression. I don't think it's because of the puke, but maybe that's part of it.

I almost forget what I'm doing, but the cramping in my hands serves as a reminder. I look back at Farber. The chest holds still, the eyes stare off at nothing like those glass eyes in creepy, old dolls.

He is gone.

I release his neck, his slimy flesh showing a ring of dark where my hands were. The cramped muscles in my fingers refuse to stop curling themselves up, so I press them flat on the floor to stretch them. I close my eyes and feel that stretch fight against the fatigue, feel the cool combat the heat of the hatred still coursing all through me.

"I'll check the circuit breaker," Glenn says from behind me.

His voice sounds all small. He's not himself. I don't open my eyes, but I nod. I hear his footsteps trail away, slow and light. He even seems to walk with hesitation now.

I know I must be in shock at this point. I guess I don't feel much just yet. If anything, I feel pleasure. I feel powerful. Someone meant me harm, snuck into my home, and I eliminated the risk. My brain gives me the huge reward that goes with that. The one people get a miniature version of when the football team they root for wins. I just got the real thing, the life or death version.

But I just killed a man, a human being. Shouldn't I feel... something else, too?

That part doesn't seem real. Not yet anyway. I guess that's what shock is. When the real things aren't real.

I lift my hands from the floor and open and close them a few times. The acute cramp pain retreats for good as I do this, leaving only the dull ache that always trails wild physical exertion like this. My fingers feel almost wrong back in the air again. They miss the cool of the floor.

Something about the floor seems so refreshing, in fact, that I can't resist. I lean over, lying down so my cheek touches the wood. It hurts for a second as I make contact – maybe he got me in the face at some point – but after that initial pain that faint numbness from the cool kicks in.

I close my eyes again. I don't think about the corpse lying near my feet. I don't think about the pool of puke congealing in the doorway. I think only of the cool pressing itself into my face, and I wish it was colder, and I wish I felt it all over.

Time passes without a sound. I don't think I could sleep just now, but a calm overtakes me. I grow ever more still inside. My thoughts go from racing to jogging to walking. My breathing slows down, my heart slows down. Eventually I drift away from reality in slow motion to some place far away from here. I feel like a balloon floating up and away from it all. The real world gets smaller and smaller.

I picture Farber hovering a spoon, force pushing it across the diner like a cutlery shot put. I remember the energy around him, the excitement in the air, the way the crowd wanted to love him and did.

Then I picture his return, his physique gone frail, coughs racking his torso. Again, the crowd responded to him on a mystical level. I could feel the despair in the room, the force that drove them to believe in him like they wanted to so badly.

Finally, I picture his face as it lies now, broken by my hands. The red draining out of him. The dead doll eyes. It hardly seems like a fitting end for such a man, even if he's more or less a total dick. It's not right, I think.

The sound of Glenn's feet trotting over the floor brings me back to reality a bit, though I leave my eyes closed for now. I hear a click and place it as him flipping the light switch.

"There we go," he says, sounding a little more like himself.

Then he gasps.

"Uh..." he says. "What did you do with him?"

I tumble the question over a few times.

"What?" I say, an odd rasp in my voice.

"You know. The, uh, dead guy," he says.

My eyes snap open. I lift my head. I hesitate for a split second before I turn. And when I do, I see exactly what I expect to see.

Farber is gone.

CHAPTER 21

With the lights on, I see the bowling ball sized hole gouged in the wall. I see the nightstand toppled, two of the legs snapped. I see a bunch of chunks in the puddle of puke that look like slices of onion.

Gross.

I look at the empty spot on the floor and picture Farber as he rested there, the broken, bleeding body. He was pretty dead at the end there as I recollect.

So... I didn't just imagine all of this, right?

"You saw him, didn't you?" I say, getting to my feet. "All of that really happened."

Glenn blinks a few times like a drunk trying to see straight. He looks like he doesn't want to be here. Seeing him shaken like this kind of weirds me out. He was always so brazen up until now. This blinking sad sack hardly seems like the guy elbowing his way through the crowd at the airport. He's all fragile now.

Soft.

"Yeah," he says. "I mean... yeah."

"And it was definitely Farber, right?" I say.

"Yeah," he says, scratching the back of his neck. "I think so."

A hard edge creeps into my voice. I can't help it.

"You think so?" I say. "What the fuck does that mean?"

"Look... it was him," he says. "It's just... This is a lot to take in, man. Just chill out."

I turn away from him to stare at the wall, like that might be enough to quell my homicidal rage. I close my eyes and try to count backwards from 10. I only make it to 8.

"I just bludgeoned and then murdered an intruder who subsequently vanished into a puff of steam," I say. "And you want me to chill out?"

Glenn blinks again.

"How about instead you stop being such a huge pussy?" I say. "Because, believe me, that would be tremendous."

I exhale all loudly through my nostrils a few times like Tony Soprano. Glenn's gaze falls to the floor. He's not even going to say anything back. I guess it's probably for the best to drop it, but...

"So Riston Farber is merely a conman, huh?" I say. "This was all just some kind of illusion, of course. Another parlor trick from that huge phony that is no threat to us, yeah?"

Glenn looks far away. I can't stop verbally abusing him. Maybe murdering someone puts you in a bad mood, especially if it somehow comes undone in a mysterious manner.

"Nothing to say?" I say. "Cause you were pretty wrong. He's obviously not a phony. He probably never was."

"No," Glenn says without looking up.

"Look, he somehow got into this room," I say. "And he somehow got out of this room. I'm going to go ahead and guess that the death I dealt upon him didn't take. So he's probably immortal or some shit at this point, too."

We fall silent a moment.

"No matter how you want to look at it," I say. "I don't think there's any way to explain any of this aside from admitting the guy has some kind of power. And admitting that you were wrong. It's not a trick."

Glenn turns and leaves the room abruptly, the wood floor groaning beneath him. Part of me wants to stay on the offensive, wants to keep after him until he admits he was wrong about this. But that part is smaller than it was. I let him go.

I sit down on the bed, my eyes still tracing outlines on the floor where the body should be. It's a weird feeling to have committed murder and then have it wiped out, at least so far as I can tell. The back and forth alleviates any feeling of guilt or whatever I might have been on the verge of feeling and replaces it with frustration at never knowing what the hell is going on.

It's nothing new, though. I never know what is happening to me.

I lie back, my head resting on a piled up section of blanket. The sheet is cool under my back, and for the first time I realize that I did all of this in nothing but boxers. Weird to kill a guy in that state of undress, but I guess I probably didn't really kill him, so it's all the same.

I look at the ceiling. Out of habit I want to go back over what played out here in my memory, run through the sequence of events, establish a timeline and assign the proper meaning to it all. My brain, however, refuses to comply. I just lie here and think of nothing. I guess it'd be hard to even sequence any of the events since it almost all happened in the dark.

Shit. I wish I hadn't been so mean to Glenn. I guess I was still full of adrenalin and hatred. I couldn't stop it from pouring out.

Red on the Inside

On cue, Glenn returns with a plastic shopping bag and a roll of paper towels. He kneels, scooping his vomit into the bag as best as he can. After ripping off three rectangles of paper towel, he dabs and swipes at the floor, throwing the dirty wad into the barf bag. He spins the roll and rips off three more paper towels.

I crane my neck to watch it all. Glenn speaks, neither of our eyes ever wavering from the vomit smear.

"We need to make sure," he says.

CHAPTER 22

The Explorer rolls by the church all slow. I wish I could say we move in silence, but this piece of shit has no muffler, so it is the opposite of silence. We gaze out the window. I guess we're hoping to catch a glimpse of Farber to confirm he's not dead. In my gut I already know he's fine. Probably not a scratch on the guy.

A few people mill around on the front steps. A guy in a red polo shirt has a stack of leaflets in his hand. The others look to be empty handed. They don't seem to take notice of our vehicle passing by at the volume of a jumbo jet, so that's good.

"So what is this?" I say.

"It's a church," Glenn says.

"I know that, dickhead," I say. "I mean, is this some kind of special event or something?"

"Yeah," he says. "Real special. I guess it's some kind of crazy cult meeting."

He has the aviators on again, so I shouldn't be surprised that he's rediscovered his smart mouth. In a way I'm glad. Anything is better than seeing Glenn turned all soft and scared. I don't like it when he becomes the vulnerable one.

"Ah," I say. "Well, that's good to know. You know, I thought you might actually have some insight into what is going on here. I mean, they don't meet in this building that frequently. It must be happening for some specific reason."

Glenn pulls the Explorer into the lot and finds a spot where we can keep an eye on the front door.

We watch a while. A trickle of people stream toward the front door where the guys on the steps greet them and red shirt hands them leaflets.

"Seriously, though," I say. "How did you find out about this?"

"I have sources," he says. "And I'm also on the League of Light email list. Got an email about it last night."

"Oh," I say. "So what are we talking here, like an ice cream social or something?"

Glenn leans this way and that way, his neck contorting in an attempt to get a better angle of the church door. I can tell he's not listening to me.

"I can't see anything," he says. "Should we go in?"

"We can't go in there," I say. "I just fought the guy to the death like an hour ago. You might remember this. It inspired regurgitation to spray out of you. Made a real mess. Dude, do you honestly not remember that?"

You want to give me mock answers to my questions, Glenn? You have no idea what I'm capable of, do you?

Glenn puffs air out of his nostrils in a way that reminds me of a bull about to impale a rodeo clown ass first on a horn. It looks like he's going to say something, but then I realize he's gritting his teeth.

I look away, avoiding eye contact as though I'm dealing with an aggressive dog instead of a man. More people file into the building. More leaflets get handed about. Nothing interesting.

The parking lot continues to collect cars as well. The spaces around us fill up, which isn't so bad as I feel like it makes us less noticeable, just one of many, you know?

When I glance back at Glenn, he stills looks more or less livid. Again, in a way I'd rather deal with enraged Glenn, his face gleaming red with blood, his mustache atwitter with a case of the shimmy shakes. It's not ideal, but it's less pathetic than scaredy-cat Glenn.

It's not until I see one of the people adjust his hat on the way in that I realize most of them are sporting head wear. He lifts his Atlanta Braves cap up and plops it back on his skull. It takes a second to register that he's not bald, or at least it wasn't male pattern baldness I saw under there. It was the weird monk haircut again. Based on the number of hats, most of these weirdos have it. Even some ladies.

"What do you think is up with the haircuts?" I say.

"I assume it's to do with the original friar reason," Glenn says. "Some kind of mystic status symbol, a sign of their commitment, of their renunciation of the ways of the world."

Weird.

I'm about to ask follow up questions when a black van creeps into the entry way of the lot. It moves slowly, with care. I guess this sticks out to both of us. We both watch it in our respective rearview mirrors as it settles into a spot in the back of the lot, away from the other vehicles. Upon parking, the van is still. No one gets out. I can't make out anything through the tinted windshield.

"Do you think?" I say.

"Maybe," Glenn says.

We wait. I can still hear some anger in the exhalations

134

emitting from Glenn's nostrils.

A man emerges from the driver's seat wearing a button-up blue shirt and one of those cabbie hats. Are those Scottish? I can't remember. He moves to the back of the van and slides open the door.

Well, well, well... look who's walking upright in a manner that I would call, "especially not dead."

Yep.

Riston Farber.

"You called it," Glenn says. "No bruises or anything."

Indeed. Farber's complexion looks unmarked. His neck lacks the purple ring of death I put there. His nose remains more pointy than flat.

He sports his usual black attire. He takes a few steps out of the van and stretches, his back arching and his arm coming up behind his head.

And then his head snaps our way. Glenn gasps as Farber squints at us and smiles. I feel that cool surge of adrenalin enter my bloodstream again, my heart beating hard like a giant kick drum. I undo my seatbelt, certain we're about to kick off Round 2 of our death match.

Then Farber snaps his head the other way and rolls his neck. The nature of these movements suggests that he was never looking at us, that he was just stretching his neck.

I'm not sure.

Either way, we can't move. Even after he goes inside the church and they close the front doors, Glenn and I sit for a long time, keeping still in the silence.

CHAPTER 23

We sit on canvas chairs on Glenn's deck. It's an unseasonably warm day, and the sun shines down like everything is normal rather than weirder than ever. When I look out at the yard and watch the light change when the clouds move, I can almost believe the lie.

I guess cleaning up all of that puke whet Glenn's appetite. As soon as we got back from the church, he made some crazy Mi Goreng flavored ramen that is probably the greatest thing I've ever tasted. The sauce coating the noodles was all spicy and acidic. Hard to describe. We didn't speak during the meal, but I think getting something to eat lifted both of our spirits.

Now we sit on the deck sipping iced tea out of a pair of mason jars. Though it's warm for a day in the late fall, the cold tea is a bit much. I'm chilly. I believe Glenn to be one of those people that wears shorts year round, however, so I'm sure he doesn't care.

I realize there's something I never told Glenn, something that got lost in the shuffle of murder undone and resurrections verified.

"I talked to her," I say.

Glenn looks confused for a fraction of a second, and then I see alertness snap into his expression.

"It worked? You saw her?" he says.

"Yes and no. I didn't see her," I say. "But I talked to her. Kind of. She was like a voice in my head I could think to."

He sips at the tea as he processes my clarification.

"What'd she say?" he says.

"She said Farber means us harm. That's why she's been trying to communicate with us," I say. "And she elaborated on why she wants to stay out there at some length."

"So she's OK?" he says.

"Yeah, she seems to like it there."

He looks away from me and nods all slow.

"Wonder why it didn't work for me," he says.

"She said it was something to do with changing sleep patterns. And she said something else, too," I say. "She said that Farber walks among us, meaning in the other world. She has seen him there and avoided him."

Glenn closes his eyes for a long moment. He slits them open, and I can see the wet in them.

"I was wrong, OK?" he says, his voice all low. "I was wrong about him. We have to get her out of there."

I don't say anything. Again, I don't know if rescuing someone that doesn't want to be rescued is our best course of action. Her reasons for staying seem well thought out enough.

Glenn clutches my arm. Our eyes lock, his expression pained. Maybe he knows what I'm thinking.

"He wants to harm us, right? Well, hurting her is the best way to harm me," he says. "He surely knows that much."

Glenn heads inside, and I sit on the deck a while by myself. It's cold, and my fingers are icy from the tip to the second knuckle from handling the jar of tea. For some reason I don't want to go inside, though. The wind blows and leaves tumble around.

Damn. I suppose Glenn is right, isn't he? It makes sense. But I wonder...

I pull my cell phone out of my pocket and press a couple of buttons.

"Hello?" Babinaux says. I hear the chatter of a crowd in the background.

"Hey, listen," I say. "This is going to sound weird, but I was wondering if you've heard anything about Farber recently. I know there was some kind of get together today, and he seemed fine, but I don't know. Anything weird going on that you know about?"

"Well, no," she says. "I'm at the church now, actually, and he's here. Like I said, I'm well out of the informed circle at this point, but I haven't detected anything out of the ordinary. Why? What happened?"

"Oh, it was nothing," I say. "He kind of appeared in my room. We struggled. I killed him with my bare hands, at which point he vanished. We checked up on him at the church a bit ago and he seemed upright and animated and full of life juice. And, you know, not dead."

"I have to go," she says, her voice hushed.

"What's wrong?" I say.

"He's staring at me," she says.

The crowd noise cuts out, and then there's silence.

I lie in the dark. Awake. I didn't bother to take the blankets off the windows, so it's a full-on dark. I guess the crack under the door lets in a sliver of light. Not enough to matter.

I decided to stay at Glenn's so we can get started early

tomorrow. He insisted I should stay. Would I be able to sleep in this room if the murder stuck? Probably not. It didn't, though, so now this room is just fine. More like a room a heated wrestling match occurred in than a killing.

I pull the lip of the blanket up over my chin and the movement wafts some of the warm under-blanket air across my face. Feels awesome. Feels like sleep.

Even so, I kind of think I won't be able to find slumber since I just went on a dream tour of the woods this afternoon. Sucks, too, cause I'm exhausted in some ways and wide awake in others. Maybe I'll break out that little black box soon. Some blue light would really hit the spot about now.

I feel dumb somehow. Embarrassed.

Embarrassed that Farber tricked us, that he's just openly taunting us, if not also trying to kill us or whatever. That guy is a dick.

I'm going to level with you. I can hardly wait to kill him again.

The murderous feeling rises from my gut, and I try to push it back down.

So here we are. I guess rage and a hateful lust for violence have replaced the level of depression that got me so down I could barely stay awake before. Not sure which is better, really. I mean, I don't feel useless like I did, but if my only use is satisfying some animal urge to eliminate a threat, I'm hardly on a fulfilling path.

Anyway.

Tomorrow we're going back. We will cut a hole in the wall and walk there.

The old fashioned way.

The dangerous way.

Glenn wants to be sure we both get there in a timely manner and together this time. He says he will take Amity by force if he must. I don't necessarily agree with this course of action, but I don't know. What if I didn't help him and Amity somehow got hurt? I'd feel like a huge jerk. It's not my place to decide these things.

I don't know if I have a place at all, really.

CHAPTER 24

I wake to the sound of the coffee grinder, that violent whir as the blade reduces beans to powder, like the noise of someone gargling gravel. I open my eyes, but with the windows covered, it's still dark as hell in here. I don't mind this. I close them, and I drift back below the surface, the surge of warmth welcoming me right back.

I hover there a while, somewhere between half and all the way asleep. Some minutes later I wake again, bobbing back up to consciousness. The coffee smell is everywhere. I'm no smellologist, but I believe this to be a dark roast, and I want some.

I rise, my feet padding over cold wood. I open the door a crack to have a little light to dress by. I know turning on the lights would only hurt after being in the dark so long.

I hear kitchen-y noises and know some special meal is being prepped. Based on what happened to Glenn last time, we might be out in the other world for months in Earth time. You don't march into that kind of shit with an empty belly.

Lord no.

Squinting in the light, I take my seat at the snack bar.

"Morning, Grobnagger," Glenn says, his back to me.

He moves food and dishes around, I think. I can't see through him, but that's an educated guess.

"Good morning," I say.

"Did you call Babinaux?" he says.

"Yep," I say.

She has been tasked with feeding Mardy while I'm away. His life is in her hands. I repeated that a few times. She didn't think it was funny.

I rest my forearms on the corner of the counter and adjust on my stool. As I do so, I feel the part of my brain that records click on like it does in those most dramatic life moments. Like when you visit a dying relative in the hospital or find a dead pet or kiss a girl for the first time.

So right now my camera films the image of the counter my face is tilted toward with my arms pressed on it. I look up to see Glenn swivel with plates. He places mine before me, dead center of the frame. His eye still looks swollen from our fight, but it looks better than it did yesterday.

The recording continues as we pile together our food stuffs and put them in our face holes. We eat a breakfast of champions, and I'm not talking about Wheaties. I speak of huevos rancheros, a Mexican dish comprised of fried eggs served on corn tortillas with tomato chili sauce, refried beans, avocado chunks and rice. Words to capture its deliciousness elude me. Let's just say it's a pretty legitimate reason to keep living.

The meal feels significant beyond that, though. I watch Glenn eat, lifting overfilled tortillas to his face, chili sauce in his mustache, chunks of egg tumbling to the plate and splatting. It all feels important. My brain records everything in high definition. Until the day I die, I will be able to call forward that image of Glenn's sauce mouth with crystal clear accuracy.

Red on the Inside

Many moments in life come and go like they never happened, but I will keep this one. A quiet breakfast.

Is this how things always feel right before a dramatic moment? A heightened awareness of your surroundings and your companions. It feels like we're going into battle or something.

I don't know why.

We're only going to walk through the wall to some other dimension. No big whoop.

CHAPTER 25

Glenn comes back from the garage with a stone bowl of black powder. Examining the bowl, I realize it's a mortar, and he probably just took a pestle to the black stuff in there. His shoes clatter on the ceramic tiles in the kitchen, and the noise changes abruptly as he moves onto the hardwood, the emphasis shifting from the slap of his feet connecting with the floor to the shifting of his weight and its ever altering strain on the planks.

"So what is this stuff?" I say, rising to follow him down the hall.

"The powder? Oh, it's just a little concoction I came up with," he says.

At this point I don't even expect him to expound. I know what this guy is playing at.

"And what are the ingredients to your concoction?" I say.

"Oh, nothing too fancy. A little chalk," he says. "And a whole bunch of don't worry about it."

Why?

Why do I even ask?

A noise startles me, a sibilant sizzle. It reminds me of an insect or maybe a small threatened animal.

Oh.

It's laughter.

He laughs at his own joke. Hard. It's one of those hissing laughs where you hear spit and air whistling between clenched teeth. Kind of gross.

"So I guess you're in pretty good spirits," I say. "I'm just glad you were able to put that embarrassing vomit episode behind you so quickly. A lot of people wouldn't be able to live something like that down for a long time, but you're not uncomfortable with being the guy that puked on the floor during a tense moment. I think that's great."

As I say it, I realize this comes off a little meaner than the light-hearted sarcasm I had intended. The pulse of his laugh slows down, but it doesn't quite stop. I guess I'm glad for that.

We enter the guest bedroom – my old sleeping grounds as I call it. My eyes can't help but check the spot on the floor for Farber's corpse even though I've seen him up and walking around. There's no body, so that's a relief, I think. It would only complicate things at this point.

Glenn sets the bowl down on the floor. He kneels next to it and pinches some of the black dust between his finger and thumb and rubs back and forth so it spills back into the bowl a little at a time. Once his fingers are empty, he does it again.

His eyes fasten on his work and twitch back and forth over it. I see great inquisitiveness in his features. Something about his expression reminds me of that curious look a bird gets as it's about to rip a nightcrawler out of the ground.

"So how does this work?" I say.

He doesn't break his eye contact with the powder between his fingers.

"Well," he says. "I do my thing, and you kind of keep quiet."

He smiles again, pleased with himself.

Why does the man delight in effing with me so? No one can say.

He reaches behind his back and pulls something out of the rear pocket of his jeans. When his hand returns to my field of vision, I see that it's a flat head screwdriver.

He pokes the tip of the tool into the black powder, taking a few stabs at the middle of the substance before he moves on to grinding the head of the screwdriver against the edge of the bowl.

Was this something like the scraping I heard back in the dark in the jail cell just before Glenn cracked open the wall? I could ask, but I'm not in the mood for a bunch of additional smart ass remarks.

The grinding sound evens out, settling into a droning loop of metal scraping against stone. You can hear the circular quality of his screwdriver stroke somehow, the rise and fall as it loops over and over.

The white noise helps me zone out from my physical surroundings. My consciousness sucks up into my head more fully, and again, I become aware that my brain is on high alert, recording the proceedings for safe keeping in my memory bank.

In fairness, something about the image is striking. A grown man kneeling before a bowl, poking a screwdriver at it? That alone doesn't inspire intrigue, maybe. It's something about the man himself.

The creases at the corners of his mouth show determination. The lines around his eyes convey the faintest squint, communicating some wordless sense of intelligence and vulnerability. His posture gives off a sense of pride beaten down a little, like some fierce animal that's been tamed and forced to jump through too many rings of fire to count. He looks so specific just now. Out of all of the people in the history of the world, there has only been one Glenn Floyd. He's a ridiculous man but an interesting and kind one, too. And I can see all of that in this moment in a way that borders on overwhelming.

Plus, his mustache is perfect.

When Glenn rises and moves to the wall, it takes my brain a second to wake from my daydream of fiery rings. He begins to scrape the screwdriver on the wall, running it up and down to chip out a line of wallpaper in the rough shape of a door. It's another vaguely familiar sound, taking me back to my time in the cell. That was a concrete wall of course, so the scrape was more rough and shrill. Grating. Still, the scraping pattern calls it to mind.

Once there's a clear doorway outlined on the wall, Glenn pulls something from his left front pocket. I can't get a good look at it as he adjusts it in his fingers, so it's small enough to be mostly obscured by hand, I guess. Significantly smaller than a breadbox. He presses it to the wall, and from what I can see, it almost looks like a silver crayon. It smears along the outline, leaving a trail of something neither slimy nor colored at all. Being close enough to see the consistency of the layer of clear smear on the wall, my best guess is that it's a piece of wax or some similar substance.

He steps back and looks over his work, leaning this way and that to get better angles. I guess maybe the wax is easier to see if you get the light to reflect off of it just so.

Just as my mind remains in record mode for all of this time, I get the sense that Glenn operates in an odd state of mind as well. He looks lost in his work, his reality filtered down to just this bowl of black sand and the rectangle etched into the wallpaper. He is no longer aware that I'm still in the room. He looks to be not entirely here himself.

He scoops up the bowl and cradles it in his left arm, hugging it to his ribs. He then sticks his right index finger in his mouth and appears to swab it on the inside of his cheek like detectives using that weird q-tip to collect DNA in every TV cop drama.

He extracts the wet finger from his maw, and I take a step back – perhaps some instinctive fear of wet willies leftover from childhood. The index finger doesn't swipe at my ear, however. It swipes at the bowl, pulling free with a bunch of black powder stuck to it. I can now see that the powder is finer than granulated sugar.

Something about all of this is pretty disgusting. I don't know. I'm no fan of fingers in mouths or saliva used as an adhesive like that. Just not my thing.

Glenn brings the finger up to his face so close that he goes cross-eyed gazing upon it. It's quite a sight, a 50-some-year-old man with a dirty finger about two centimeters rom the tip of his nose. And there's such a sense of reverence in the silence around us now, all anticipation and wonder and just a glimmer of amazement.

The words blurt out of me:

"Checkin' the ol' dipstick, eh?"

I'm not even sure what I'm saying until I'm done talking. In the silence, I run it back in my memory.

148

Red on the Inside

And then I laugh. The kind of laugh that brings tears to your eyes within seconds. The kind of laugh that shakes your ribcage so hard, it makes it damn near impossible to breathe. The kind of laugh that stretches out in front of you like it could never possibly end. The kind of laugh that makes you feel like a different person.

I'm not sure why this level of laugh has come upon me. I mean, I don't know if it's that funny. It must be something about this moment, this tension settling over the room.

Glenn looks at me for those first few seconds, and then he laughs, too. Almost as hard as me.

I watch the world through the blur of teared up eyelashes opened just enough to see through. We laugh a long time, I think. Glenn laughs harder when I laugh harder, and I have this crazy disconnected feeling like we aren't even laughing at the same thing that somehow makes it that much funnier.

This goes on for a while. First, I bend at the waist, and then I kneel on the floor. A flash of heat comes over my face.

I start punctuating my laughing jags with deep breaths, trying to get back under control.

Each time I gather the poise necessary to slow the flood of laughter, my eyes dart to that black powder finger just sitting there on its own, pointing at the ceiling, and that image somehow makes the whole thing seem funny again.

The dipstick itself.

Glenn sets the bowl down on the bed and pulls up the collar of his t-shirt to wipe his eyes. He takes a few deep breaths and seems to gather himself.

This self control must be infectious to some degree. My laughter keeps rolling, but it has lost some of its intensity.

Gathering the bowl once more, Glenn moves to the wall. He smears his black powder finger along the wax line. I watch, laughter still twitching up from my gut in little fits.

And I hear something, the tiniest sound. It almost sounds like the rubber seal peeling away as a fridge door opens. What the hell was that?

I sit forward, no longer laughing, ass scooted to the very edge of the mattress.

He keeps working, really rubbing his finger into the wall. I begin to see the first area he coated with black soot, except it's not just coated with black soot. The spot recesses into the wall. Not a lot. Maybe a quarter of an inch.

The fridge sound emits from the crack again as he dips his finger back into the bowl. Will he have to lick it again? Will he have to use a different finger? Neither. He curls the index finger and spoons up some powder, half flinging to the wall before he goes to grinding at it. Clouds of black billow to the ground. Sloppy as hell, this fool.

Looking back at the wall, I see that more of the line has blackened and recessed. I guess that process must produce the opening fridge door noise.

He works faster now, and it seems like the black wants to stick to the line. Some of it spills to the floor, sure, but the bulk of it seems to leap from his finger and adhere itself to the wall. And then it settles for a bit and does that lip popping fridge thingy.

Weird shit.

Glenn squats to finish the very bottom of each side, which he makes short shrift of, and then stands. He almost brushes his finger against his shirt but thinks better of it.

"I'm going to get cleaned up," he says. "Are you ready to go?"

I consider this for a moment.

"I think I'm ready," I say.

CHAPTER 26

Just like in the jail cell, Glenn wedges his fingers into the recessed area and wiggles the door out a little at a time. I see the white light shine through the crack as he finagles the section of wall. He gives me a nasty look, so I go to help him.

Behind the facade of wallpaper, the door looks like smooth stone about four inches deep. I get my fingers around it and we pull. It's sort of like moving a smaller version of one of those blocks at Stone Henge. For some reason all I can think about is how it'd be that much more of a bitch on carpeted floor. I don't even know if that's true, but it seems like it. I picture the corner catching on the fibers over and over.

We grunt and heave and lift with our backs, and soon it's open a decent amount. I move to do more pushing than pulling now that there's a little room to do so. I turn to get a better look behind the door as I take my new position, just glancing at it out of the corner of my eye as the push continues. The light spills into the room through the eight inch opening, bright and white and eyeball scorching. It dapples over my arms as they strain against the block.

"Don't look directly into it," Glenn says.

Immediately, I look directly into it.

I don't really see anything, though. Just some whiteness and what not. Illumination and all. It burns pink spots onto my retinas that seem to flutter about my field of vision.

"Let's focus on getting this open," he says. "You'll have time to look into the light when we're done."

He sounds so much like a dad reasoning with a toddler that I feel bad. I turn back, and we toil some more and exert ourselves and the doorway lurches forward an inch or so at a time.

I notice that the corner of the block is gouging a pretty good scratch into the wood floor. I wonder if this will disappear or something when we walk through. I'd ask Glenn, but I don't want him to blow a damn gasket when he sees how fucked his floor is. I imagine he feels the same way about the floors as he does about the leather in the Explorer, if not touchier still.

"That's good," he says, and we stop inching the door open.

We stand a moment, hands on hips, chests both huffing and puffing. I look at the light for as long as I can stand it. Pretty bright. I grab my hoodie and pull it on.

"Well," I say. "Let's go."

Glenn nods, and he steps forward toward the door, then stops.

"Oh my dear God," he says, mumbling.

"What?"

He clutches at his chest as though he's having a heart attack.

"Just look what we've done to the floor."

CHAPTER 27

We walk into the light.

"Just keep moving forward," Glenn says. "I'll be right behind you."

I step through the doorway, eyes squinted to slits. The light surrounds me, shocking in its intensity. It gets at my eyes and stings a little, but I'll be OK.

By the time I've taken two more steps, I can see nothing but the brightest light. I turn back to get a look into the guest bedroom from this vantage point out of curiosity, but I guess I was too slow. There's only light in all directions now. No door. No Glenn. Just light.

"Keep moving forward," I say to myself, echoing Glenn's advice.

Yep. I do that. Forward, I move.

I see now that there's a blue tint to the light. It looks white from afar, maybe out of sheer brightness, but there's a blue undertone when you're inside of it. Weird.

I realize that I have no feel for how far I've gone now or how fast I'm moving. The light drowns out my sense of these things.

And suddenly squinting is not enough. The light attacks me, forces itself onto me. The sting swells into a sharp pain, stabbing ice picks of blazing glow into my head. I go to close my eyes and shield them with my hands, but it makes no difference.

I run. I plaster my hands over my eyes and run, but it's no use. The light pushes its pointy fingers into my skull, jabs them into my brain.

I want to scream, but I can't muster it. The stabby feelings in my head make all of my facial and neck muscles tense up and writhe in a way that makes vocalizing impossible. I can't even open my mouth. I can sort of hum, if I push from the diaphragm.

So I do that. I hum the sounds of anguish the best I can. I hum the hum of the stabby brained. Let's just say it's not the most beautiful of melodies.

I stumble on my own feet and belly smack the ground. I go to hop up right away, but I freeze. The pain is too much to concentrate on other things now. I slink back down. All I can do is picture blood gushing out of my eye sockets, the red streaming down in two rivers.

And then something gives. Some unexplained shift happens, and I'm OK. The brightness fails to dim even the slightest bit, but it doesn't matter now. It doesn't hurt me anymore.

I rise, and I press forward like Glenn would want.

As I walk deeper and deeper into the light, my thoughts seem to simplify: I am warm. I like the warm. It is bright here. That is OK, too. Sometimes the warm and the bright seem to go together, like the sun. I like the sun. It is warm.

I like blankets. They are soft. They get warm if you wait.

I keep shaking my head, and that seems to reset my brain back to dim as opposed to extremely dim.

And I walk, and the light dissolves around me, and it's like I'm walking through fog. Or like maybe Amity set up a kickass smoke machine to make our entrance more dramatic. That'd be pretty sweet. Like any second now a voice will say, "Ya'll ready for this?" and the beat will drop. Glenn and I will rush onto the scene and do some kind of awesome high five move, probably one of those elaborate high fives with a bunch of steps involved, in fact.

Yep.

Any second now...

Tendrils of mist coil and reach out toward me, and I feel a chill creep into the air. Even through my hoodie, goosebumps wriggle across my arms. At first I think it's that rush of cool that runs through you when things are exciting, such as when the beat is about to drop. But no. It's cold as hell here. Dead of winter cold.

The fog sinks frosted teeth into my skin where it makes direct contact, and my skin feels all dry like it's cracking from the cold.

Maybe Amity opted for a shitload of dry ice instead of a smoke machine, 'cause what the hell? It's chilly.

Starting to miss the bright and warm feeling of walking in the light earlier, even if it tried to burn out my eyeballs for a while there.

I keep expecting the fog to clear and the green woods to appear any second now. I bet it's much warmer there. The woods are always nice and warm. Not too hot. No. Just a real nice temp.

Not like this. This is like walking around in a deep freezer.

I pull my arms in from the sleeves of my hoodie and hug

them against me. Thankfully I'm wearing a t-shirt underneath, as I briefly make the mistake of touching the ball of my thumb to my neck. Frigid.

I try to pick up the pace, but it's hard. The cold makes me want to quit. Every step turns into a battle, but I keep going, keep putting one foot in front of the other, keep kicking into the fog.

Even so, the cold only advances. It edges up my legs and lurks around the perimeter of my torso, waiting for the opportunity to stab icicles all through my core.

Is the fog a touch brighter now? It's hard to tell. It seems like I can see some brighter white gleaming through.

The muscles in the trunk of my body spasm and shudder, and now I'm shivering. The violent shakes only slow me down, though. I can't help but get mad each time my body jerks without my say so. I just want to walk until this is over, and my body is fighting me.

My teeth begin to chatter, so I hold my mouth a little open so they won't bang into each other. My jaw can just wiggle away and make its own fun.

So yeah.

It's cold.

I watch my feet disappear into the fog over and over as I walk. I try to think of nothing but that: the next step and the next, but tears drip from my nose. My body spews water from my tear ducts into my nasal cavity to try to fight the dryness, but it only makes the cold sting worse.

And then my foot doesn't vanish into the clouds. It meets a touch of resistance as it descends, and there's a familiar crunch as it continues landing.

Snow.

I look up to see an utter lack of fog. In its place I find not the green woods I was expecting, but a frozen landscape. Sparsely wooded fields of snow sprawl in all directions, with flatlands to my right and hills to my left. Maybe it's just in contrast to the snow, but the trees all look black. They're probably just leafless for the winter, but it's hard to imagine they're not dead. Crunchy stalks of grass gone beige poke up from the white in patches. They seem like the only thing around that's not a shade of black or white.

No Glenn? I sort of thought we'd come out of there right together? Wait. Maybe he's not through yet. I was a few paces ahead of him after all, and I'm generally a pretty fast walker.

I don't know. Should I wait around or something?

I pace back and forth a little, moving to try to keep warm as I mull it over. With my arms crossed over my chest inside my hoodie, I rub my hands on my upper arms. Friction seems like a good idea, but everything is numb enough now that I can't really tell the difference.

This snow doesn't fluff or billow as I march through it. It's too crisp for all of that. My shoes break it time and again. It sort of sounds like someone eating cereal all slow.

Ah. There we go.

Footprints form a path trailing up over the biggest hill to my left. It looks like one set of prints, so I'll assume it's Glenn. Admittedly the snow is torn up to the degree that it's plausible these could be the footprints of more than one person walking single file. Let's not forget that Glenn is on the heavyset side, though. He could really tear up some snow if he put his mind to it.

I trudge along the path. Weirdly, it may be tougher going in this loosened snow than it was on the crisp stuff. Hm... That's dumb.

Wait. I guess I could just walk next to the path.

Yep. It's genius. I feel like Albert Einstein and myself are men of similar ilk.

I tread along next to the path. It's still difficult to make my way up the hill – the incline is on the steep side - but at least I can get a little traction in the crunchiness.

I climb a while. It's so still out here. No sounds but those of my shoes collapsing snow bits. It always seems quieter when there's snow, I guess. I think it dampens the sound.

I step on an icy patch and slip, landing on one knee.

Shit.

I stand and shimmy an arm back into its sleeve to brush the snow off of my pants. Most of it comes off, but there's a decent sized wet spot.

So that's good.

My hand stings worse than before from touching the wet. I wiggle it back under the hoodie blanket and go back to the friction efforts which may or may not be working. Thinking back, I'm lucky I didn't fall flat on my face with my arms tucked in like this.

I resume the climb, really digging to make the final few steps.

There.

As soon as I top the hill, I make eye contact with Glenn. He stands in front of a pine tree, his hands folded neatly in front of him. Well, well, well... That was a little easier than I thought it might be. I pictured myself trekking a long way as I usually do out here.

But then I notice that he doesn't look happy to see me. He closes his eyes and shakes his head, disappointed. And I realize that his hands aren't folded in front of him. They're bound.

Movement to his left catches my eye. Ah, now I see that he's not alone. Three men stand just behind him, black cowls shrouding their heads. Between the hoods and the fact that they're partially obscured by pine boughs, I can't get a great look at them.

I squint to study them, waiting for the faces to come into the clear. It seems they haven't spotted me yet. I'll just get a better look really quick and then hide.

But I don't make it past the first face. My mouth drops open. My brain shuts down.

Riston Farber.

CHAPTER 28

Snowy hills stretch out before us. Black trees jut from the white here and there, holding their arms up like someone might see them and come pluck them from the cold. Part of me thinks this might be worth a shot, but a piece of rope binds my hands together now. I feel like you need to get those arms out wide if you really want someone to save you, and my ability to do so is hindered.

I mean, who's going to rescue some guy that's making a letter I with his body rather than a Y? I'm sorry, but that's just not how this works.

Glenn and I walk ahead of the others, I guess so they can keep an eye on us. Farber, Cromwell and Woods comprise our captors – the three amigos, as no one calls them. So far Farber has yet to speak. Woods does most of the talking. I've tried to search Cromwell's face for signs of sympathy or friendship, but he won't look at me for more than a second. When he does, his expression conveys no feelings, good or bad. I'm not sure what to make of that.

On the other hand, Farber stared holes through me when they first came upon me. He paced a semi-circular path in front of me while my hands were bound, his eyes never leaving my face. I expected to see some glee there, some gloating smile in his eyes at having caught us, but I saw no sadistic pleasure. I saw a hard expression, a permanent crinkle between his eyebrows. Instead of demonic joy, I found intensity, coldness, perhaps a hint of mild disappointment conveyed in his features.

"Veer left about 45 degrees," Woods says, cupping a hand to his mouth. "We'll cut right between those two trees."

He points, and Glenn and I follow the trajectory of his finger, blazing a trail in the snow. Woods is a small man with fat cheeks. He appears to be older than the other two. There's a tired look about him, a droop to his eyes and a sag to his cheeks. He seems like someone's dad that just wants to be left alone so he can put on his slippers, kick back in his recliner, and watch sports on TV 365 nights a year without speaking a word to anyone. Instead he's out here directing foot traffic on some astral plane, probably missing the big game as we speak.

I submitted to my capture peacefully. I was ready to run for it, but Glenn said I should just do what they say. I see now that Woods wears a scabbard with a handle sticking out of it. I'm going to go way out on a limb here and suggest that perhaps there's a blade connected to that hilt. Anything is possible. I'm guessing Glenn's insistence that I give in had to do with not wanting me to get stabbed, an impulse I can appreciate and endorse wholeheartedly.

Reading between the lines of the conversation as they apprehended me, apparently Glenn had told them he was traveling alone, and they believed him. They were surprised to see me. Pleased, too. If I had just hidden a moment sooner instead of standing there like a fool...

We walk for a long time, passing through the gap between the pair of trees Woods mentioned. The snow grows deeper as we advance, tougher to trudge through, and it slows us down.

It occurs to me that the wintry landscape surrounding us is likely permanent rather than seasonal, or at least that would make sense. I remember Glenn talking about how time seemingly doesn't pass in these places. It's daylight forever in this part, nighttime forever in that part. So maybe this is the forever winter part? I think that's probably right. Not a great place to call home. Not that great to visit either, really.

The march continues, our footsteps crunching out a pulsing rhythm like a sleepy drum beat where the snare always hits a touch late. I don't know if it's the sound or the cold that lulls me into that far away feeling. Maybe it's a little of both.

In any case, my thoughts begin to percolate. As the shock of all of this fades away, an interesting mix of anticipation and dread ripple all through me. I feel like something important is about to happen, and yet I'm not as scared as I probably should be considering my last encounter with Farber as well as Amity's warning about him.

Up close and personal like this, he seems less like the evil figure that I had envisioned and more like a really focused, intense guy. He may well mean us harm, but it's not in that cruel, Freddy Krueger way. It's something else. It's like the difference between being scared of a person breaking into your house compared to a bear passing by the cabin you're staying in. Both are terrifying, but you know the bear has no malicious intent. Even if it attacks you, it's because it's a simple creature that doesn't know any better. The guy breaking into your house, however? Evil dick. Him you have total contempt for.

Even so, I'm not that scared for now. I just have this feeling that we're going to slip out of this like we always seem to. I don't know. Maybe it's like after you dread something for a long time, as it's happening it doesn't seem that bad in a way, because at least the dread is over.

As we walk on, the land flattens out into total desolation. No trees. No signs of any life. Just a flat expanse of untouched snow. A tundra that seems to stretch on forever.

Am I excited to see where we're going? Maybe a little. Is this what Cromwell meant when he said you feel like anything is possible when Farber is around? I guess I can see it. Even when you're his prisoner, you feel like something massive is about to go down.

I watch gusts of wind flutter frozen powder this way and that. I think my body temp goes down a few degrees just from looking at it.

My arms, legs, and face are so numb now that the cold doesn't bother me that much, though. A dull ache persists everywhere instead of sharp pains in the coldest places like before. It's not pleasant, but it's not too bad. And my core stays reasonably warm from the aerobic exercise anyway, or at least I think that's what's happening. Maybe the chill is merely calming my thoughts before it shuts off the lights for good. I understand that hypothermia is a smooth talker. It soothes you right up until the end.

I don't know. Pretty sure if I keep moving, I'll be fine, though.

My thoughts sink below the surface level of sensory details again and forage around in the feelings part. Even if I'm mostly not panicking about my predicament, one bit of uneasiness still resides down there in the murky bits – a twinge of genuine, pants-shitting fear emitting from one detail: Cromwell's lack of eye contact. I don't like it. That's probably the one thing that makes me worry that this whole thing will turn out the wrong way.

I think back to his demeanor in his apartment. He seemed so much the type to be himself under any circumstances, to do so to a fault by annoying people with his honesty. There's a fine line between candor and obnoxiousness that I figured Cromwell crossed with gusto like it was a finish line on a regular basis. I just can't imagine him being too discrete about anything, you know?

And then he gave me that gesture to tell me to get out of the church when Farber made his triumphant return. So he was into helping me at that point.

Something has changed, though. He sure isn't helping me now. But is he playing it all cold to conceal his feelings from me or from Farber? Hard to say.

A creaking sound beside me shakes me back to reality. It's Glenn gasping almost under his breath, his eyes gone wide. I follow his gaze out into the snowy distance.

There's something there, a darker shade set in the white, maybe a structure of some kind. It takes my eyes a second to make sense of it. I see columns set in a circle with a platform in the center of them. It's hard to get a sense of scale, but it almost looks like a gazebo with no roof.

The men mumble behind us. I glance back to see Woods pointing and Farber nodding. I can't understand them, but I take it that they've spotted the gazebo as well. I look upon Cromwell for a while, but he stares at the ground.

I turn back and we walk on, the structure seeming to grow as we draw near.

165

"What is it?" I whisper.

"An altar," Glenn says.

CHAPTER 29

So the roofless gazebo is a little bigger than I thought. The marble floor forms a circle about the size of a basketball court. There's no snow coating it, not even a little, nor is there any white stuff on the matching marble platform in the center of it. I guess that's the actual altar now that I think about it. Anyway, it doesn't look like the snow has been cleared from these surfaces. It looks like there never was any there. I guess that's hard to say definitively, but that's what it looks like.

We walk toward the altar, our feet moving with ease in silence that is shocking after so long battling at the crunchity crunch out there.

"Sit," Woods says, pointing.

As soon as Woods commands Glenn and I to take a seat on the altar, I know two things: it's a matter of time before the cold freezes me solid now that I'll be sitting still on a stone slab, and we're probably about to perform some ritual which may or may not involve a human sacrifice of a guy with a consonant stuffed last name that rhymes with Throbdagger.

Yep. So things are looking up.

We sit.

"I don't suppose you guys have any blankets," I say.

No one even cracks a smile, so I learn right away that this is a tough crowd. Glenn elbows me in the ribs and shakes his head. He always gets uptight in moments like these, but I don't see how talking could make any difference now.

The hooded men look at each other and then back at me.

"You're just a kid," Farber says.

His voice sounds thinner than I had imagined. It's not squeaky or anything like that. Just kind of a normal, intelligent tone. I guess I figured him for a deep, thick voice like a lich lord or something.

"I don't know," I say. "I'm 27."

Air puffs out of his nostrils, and in the cold, it looks like smoke.

"That may be so," he says. "You're fully grown. You've existed for the time necessary to become a man. But you think and live like a child that knows nothing. Out here? This place? It has given you a gift that you don't know how to accept."

I don't say anything. He paces a little as he talks. Woods' eyes watch my face, a curious look to them. Cromwell only stares at Farber, his face expressionless.

"Because, like a child, you see the world only within a framework of achieving happiness," Farber says. "You try to reconcile how this gift will fit into your pursuit of happiness instead of seeing it for what it is."

He brushes a gloved hand on one of the pillars and turns his hand over to observe it.

"Only fools speak of happiness. Only children," he says. "Men speak of power. Fools see power as an idea to be interested in or disinterested in, perhaps even an inconvenience to their dreams of happiness. Men see how power is inevitable and concrete. If ignored, it doesn't go away. Someone will possess it one way or another. Someone will use it to bend reality to their will whether you're interested or not. Power and what it's used for are what's real. They're the only things that are real. Happiness, or a lack thereof, is the inconvenience to what really matters. Or at least that's often the case."

He looks at me again and tilts his head to the side. I can't decide if there's some sympathy in his body language. I kind of doubt it.

"A man with an absence of interest in power is like man with an absence of interest in breathing," he says. "It is obtuse, unnatural, unsustainable. It fails to grasp the primal, the essence of being human."

I say nothing. Whatever is left of the body heat in my legs drains into the marble through my hamstrings. The cold reaches up through me now, finally sinking into the core of my body.

"I'm right about you, aren't I?" he says. He spreads his arms out wide, upturned palms gesturing to the sky. "Heaven gave you these gifts. It brought you here. It showed you miracles. You. Out of everyone, it loved you. It wanted you. It chose you. And you've spent your days mulling how that fit into your happiness, have you not? Perhaps it even made you sad. Think about that. A miracle that made you sad."

He smiles, and for the first time I get just a glimmer of that demonic fervor I expected to find. Perhaps it's not one of his primary personality traits, but there's a little in there after all.

"Isn't that the most adolescent thing you can imagine? A grown man that has never experienced real hunger, never experienced real pain, never experienced much of anything at all, finds a way to make a gift a burden, a way to make a miracle a tragedy."

His smile fades. I just stare into his eyes. I try not to shiver because it makes me feel weak.

"You know, real suffering exists in the world. There are babies born that starve to death before they ever learn to walk or speak. Rape. Murder. The worst abuses you can imagine are happening somewhere right now. You know what can change those things? Power. Power is the only force that can change reality. Everything else is dreaming. Escape. Selfish, delusional bullshit. Awful teenage poetry scrawled in a notebook."

My primary interest at this point is smashing his face in so he will see that I understand how power works on one of the most primal levels - the "my fist shuts your mouth" level.

My hands are so cold. I bet hitting him would really hurt. It'd be worth it and all, but still.

"This place loves you. It's connected to you. I always thought it liked me best. I thought I was special, but it is different with you," he says. "Whether it's spiritual or energy we can connect to or a little of both, it connects with you the deepest of all. And you don't care. You could change the world, and you don't care."

He clears his throat, one of those disgusting bursts of phlegmy vibrations.

Gross.

"You got nowhere on your own," he says. "Why do you think you went through all of those rituals? Culminating with the fire in the well and your resurrection? I put you through a sped up version of all of the lessons I learned. I made you more and more powerful, because you were too dumb and too selfish to see what you had. You didn't even know what was happening. Never had a clue until after you were killed and reborn."

He goes to clear his throat again, but it turns into a cough this time. A hacking, wet cough that reminds me how frail he is. It's harder to tell with the robe and hood on.

When he resumes talking, his voice sounds a little raspy from the coughing fit.

"But you and your friend will be made useful in the end. One way or the other, you will serve power just as we all do, whether we want to or not. You will serve a force greater than yourself."

Farber looks over my head and nods. I see movement out of the corner of my eye, and then something heavy bashes into the back of my head.

What?

Not cool.

I'm falling over onto my side. The words, "brain not work right," occur to me as the darkness descends, but there's something important hovering at the edge of my fading consciousness. There's something I need to remember now before it's too late.

Yes.

I know what to do.

CHAPTER 30

I let myself pour out of that spot between my eyebrows like Amity showed me. That feeling comes over me again, like there's all of this pressure focused on that one area, like water spiraling down the drain just there, except up. This time I keep my eyes open for the duration of the process. I rise slowly, inching up but not quite out of my head yet.

Everything goes the rest of the way black, though.

Shit.

Did I not get out in time? Did unconsciousness beat me to it? I try to fight it, try to push myself back to the surface.

Am I still here?

My vision fades in, a yellow tint to everything at first, and I realize that the pressure is gone. I feel free. I float skyward in slow motion. I try to look down, to see what they're up to, but I can't move. My focus won't shift anywhere else. I can look only at the sky, a gray mass of cloud-like fluff that looks more poised to go black than I had been aware of until now.

The paralysis I'm experiencing fails to scare me, though. I suspect it won't last long. I think everything is still coming around, like rebooting a computer.

Cromwell strides into my frame of vision. He opens his robe and tucks a blackjack in his pocket. Never thought I'd get knocked out by one of those, especially out here on the astral plane. I guess you never know where your life will lead until you get there.

He kneels through me, which is a weird sensation. He's down there a while, fumbling about below where I can see, presumably checking on my body. I hear noises, something scraping or sliding.

My repeated attempts at moving finally find purchase. I swivel to see Cromwell with his arms looped under my arms. He drags my body away from me. My chin rests on my chest, bobbling with every step, my neck as limp as a piece of spaghetti.

"Leave him," Farber says.

Cromwell stops walking, lets my shoulders lean back into his knees. His forehead wrinkles up.

"But I thought..." Cromwell says.

"Leave him," Farber says again. "He can wait until we go back. We'll do this one here and the second on the other side. Doing one on each side should heighten the effects."

Cromwell eases my torso to the ground. He moves with care, but the back of my head thuds into the marble still, and the man maneuvering my body grimaces at this. He bites the middle finger of his glove to pry it off quickly and feels around the back of my skull. His fingers come back clear. I'm not bleeding. So things could be worse between Cromwell and me, I figure. At least he doesn't laugh at the thought of cracking my head open like an egg. It's a start.

I turn to find Glenn's body face down on the marble. I guess he got the blackjack treatment as well. His face angles away from me, so I begin floating over there to get a look. Before I even get close, Farber and Woods come along and stoop to hoist Glenn by his armpits and ankles. They shuffle toward the altar with him.

There's mumbling as they line him up parallel with the long side of the platform. Then they sway his body back and forth, counting aloud in unison:

"One.

Two.

Three."

On three, they toss his limp body onto the stone. He wobbles there, tipping onto his side and flopping face down, but now his visage points toward me. His expression looks solemn but fine, like he's deep asleep, perhaps having a mildly disturbing dream.

Only an unconscious human being lies face down with their arms pinned underneath them. It doesn't look right. His shoulders slump oddly, and his face appears to be pressed down a little too flat somehow, like without the arms positioned to support some of the weight, it all grinds the face into the marble. It reminds me of pictures I've seen of people gunned down in the street.

I inch closer, but I'm so slow. Farber steps forward and puts a hand over Glenn's eyes. He speaks, but it's all quiet, almost a whisper, and I can't make out the words. My progress reminds me of a turtle riding a glacier, but as I draw near I can make out a syllable here and there. I think Farber is speaking Latin.

He finishes his chant, and all three men bow their heads. I move forward in the silent moment, but I'm still a good 15 feet out.

And for the first time, I'm scared. All the way scared. This has never quite felt real, I think. Even now, it's off, but I get that something bad is happening. Something really bad. It never really sank in until this long, quiet spell fell upon us like a blanket, this elongated bit of pure anticipation, a last gasp of how things are that will soon be undone.

I know something permanent is about to happen. Something that can't be taken back. I know that my life will be divided into segments after this. One segment before this moment. One segment after. I know that it will change me. I can feel all of these things.

And I can do nothing to change any of it. I can only move closer and closer to Glenn's place on the altar at the speed of an inch worm.

The men stir, the moment of silence reaching its endpoint. From my vantage point, I can see only the back of Farber's hood. Cromwell and Woods face my direction, though. They look at each other, grave expressions etching hard lines on their foreheads and around their mouths.

Farber's head bobs. That is the sign. He gives no verbal command. He doesn't have to. He can speak without moving his lips. His legion acts at his slightest gesture, his bodily whim. He commands life and death with a wink, a nod, a wave of the hand.

Woods ducks down, fiddling with something underneath the altar. Stone grinds against stone, and then the sound cuts off. Did he open something? I can't see from here, but it sounded like something of that variety.

He reaches in with one hand and then the other, presumably pulling something free, but the marble platform blocks my view. He turns to Cromwell, extends both hands. Cromwell takes the offering. I get a momentary glimpse. I

175

think I know now, but I could be wrong. I could be wrong.

Woods reaches in again, first with his left, then his right. Stone grinds on stone once more. He stands. Another glimpse, a metallic reflection flaring my way. I don't know. I could still be wrong.

And the men lean over Glenn like babysitters checking on a napping baby. They tilt their heads, their eyeballs running up and down his sprawled figure, sizing him up.

And I know. I already know. I should stop moving closer, but I can't. I should back away. I should disappear completely, just disintegrate into a cloud of dust and blow away over the tundra.

I do none of these things. I inch toward Glenn's face, my progress as slow and steady as ever.

Woods steps forward. He stands up a little straighter, raises his right hand into view. I wasn't wrong.

I can only watch now. I can only watch.

The first sword enters the left hamstring. The tip pierces the pant leg and glides through the meat, seemingly finding little resistance. There's a metallic clink as the blade meets the marble. A little blood comes, but not much. The sword plugs most of the hole.

Woods releases the hilt, and the sword stands on its own. It looks like some illusion from a magician's act, something you'd see in the circus, but it's real. I look on Glenn's face, expecting him to wake up screaming any second, but he doesn't move.

The second sword enters the small of the back, just off center, to the left of the spine. His jacket rides up, and the navy blue t-shirt pulls taut in the area surrounding the point of entry and then relaxes into wrinkles as the incision is made.

Now Cromwell steps up for his turn. He looks a little somber, though not as disturbed as you might imagine.

The third and fourth blades find homes in the lower back as well. They enter at odd angles compared to those placed by Woods, which both ran parallel to the spinal column.

Woods finds gaps between ribs to insert the fifth and sixth blades, and Cromwell does the same for the seventh and eighth, though he must also avoid the shoulder blades.

Number nine sinks into that ball of muscle that connects the neck and shoulders. And Woods pushes the tenth blade into the back of Glenn's neck. He works at it a little as this is toned and fibrous compared to the rest.

A sound like a single throaty snore comes from Glenn's throat as the metal penetrates his wind pipe. Woods unhands the hilt of the tenth blade, and we all just watch.

Ten blades stick out of Glenn's back. For now, he continues breathing. He lives. But it won't be long.

Am I in shock? I must be. I must be. I wait for the reality to sink in. Maybe none of this can be real until he is gone.

His breath rasps on, scraping in and out like he's inhaling steel wool instead of oxygen. The red spills out of him, the largest volume flowing from his neck, but it's slower than you'd think. It will take him a long time to bleed out.

He doesn't appear too upset. It is peaceful in that sense. His face shows no signs of pain. His lips still display the faintest downward curl at the corners like he's still walking through the same vaguely unpleasant dream as before. He has no clue how much worse reality has become. And I'm glad for that. I'm glad he doesn't know.

And I find parts of my brain rejecting all of this out of

hand. Wild animal parts that flail against this as a concept. How can this be the end of Glenn's story? How can he die? He is a large man, a strong man. He gets all pushy and takes what he wants from the world. He knows his way around life, knows what matters to him. He says, "What the fuck?" to the grocery store clerk that ignores him and elbows people in the back to fight through the crowd at the airport. He tried so hard to point me toward the light, tried so hard to help me see myself and my life with clarity.

He was never supposed to die. It doesn't make sense.

And I am close now. I am right next to him. Right next to his face.

Respiration inflates his chest. He doesn't stir beyond that. His features are calm and striking.

I'm not sure how long I watch him. It feels like a long time, but I can't say that with any certainty.

But his breathing slows down now, becomes more strained. The wind groans on the way in and rasps on the way out. The hesitation between each exhale and inhale grows longer and longer. And it's too long.

A final sigh emits from his lips and seems to shatter all of his bulk at once. He is smaller now.

Shrunken. Spent. Drained.

Forever.

CHAPTER 31

Please, God, erase me. Undo my creation like I was never real.

Just help me disappear.

I don't care how. I don't.

Burn me. Bury me. Cover me in dirt.

Just take me out of this place, this life.

I don't belong here. I never did.

CHAPTER 32

I wake. The sound fades in first. The quiet. The sound of the open air of the outdoors dampened by a thick shroud of snow. Muffled. A filtered version of how it's supposed to sound outside.

It is cold. It is a cold world.

I open my eyes to see the gray sky above me with columns of stone evenly spaced at the periphery of my vision. Glancing down at my body reveals my location: I lie on the marble slab where Cromwell left me. The memory of that image flashes across my mind, my head thudding against the stone and him ripping off his glove to check for blood or skull fracturing or whatever.

I blink and look back up. Is the sky going black before my eyes? It seems like it, it seems darker now, but I'm not sure.

I sit up.

The body still lies there, the swords sticking out of it. It looks posed, almost cheesy like something in one of those awful serial killer movies.

This is real, though. This is my friend. Or was. I want to cover him up. It feels like he's out in the open, exposed for everyone to see, and covering him, that will keep him safe. He looks all small now, defeated and deflated, but he's mostly the same, like he'll wake up any second now.

The cells that comprise Glenn's biological makeup are all still there for the most part. His brain is still there. His organs are still there. It doesn't make sense. All the pieces are still there. How can you turn those parts off and never be able to turn them back on? They are the same as they were before, mostly. They are the same cells, the same material. But the magical juice that made him alive is gone now. That's how it works.

He will never come back, and there will never be another Glenn Floyd.

I burst into tears. My face goes all red and hot. And I twitch in my chest and arms. I think the spasms come over me out of attempts to stop crying, out of feeling powerless and small and trying to stop it physically somehow. I try to squirm away from the overwhelming sadness and anger that racks sobs from my throat without my say so. I try to hold myself still and stop the water from pouring from my eyes.

I try these things, and I fail.

It's not fair.

Why? Why is he gone? Why does this happen? Why are we all brought here to die? Why would anyone bring us here to kill us all one by one? Who would want to hurt us like this? Why would anyone want that? What purpose could any of this serve? Why do we exist at all just to be wiped out?

Why would the universe work this way?

And consoling words erupt in my imagination.

"Death is a part of life."

Shut up. Stop trying to tell me how to fucking feel. My friend is gone. This one individual is gone forever. That the same fate befalls everyone doesn't make it any less real or any less tragic every single time. So shut it. Just leave me alone.

"He's in a better place."

Fuck off. You don't know anything. How do you know where he is? I don't need you to patronize me, talking like you know more than me when you don't know anything. Believe it or not, it doesn't comfort me to have people condescend to me, to have people talk to me in childish terms. Just because you're a coward that can't look at shit honestly, trying to put death in some box to make it seem smaller, trying to label it in some way to make it make sense to your dim brain so you don't have to think about it too hard, so you don't ever have to feel confused. But I am confused because I see it all for the mess it really is. I don't pretend I can spout some platitude that makes all the ugliness inside of me go away, all the ugliness in a universe that murders everyone and everything in time.

If you were honest with yourself, you would see it the same way. If you weren't scared to death of your own feelings, you would see how massive this is, you would feel how big it hurts. You wouldn't get all uptight. You wouldn't be so concerned about snuffing out my emotions, just as I don't care about extinguishing yours.

Nobody knows anything, so stop trying to boil it down into a bullshit slogan that will make you feel safe. It doesn't make you safe to dumb everything down like that. It just makes me think you're dumb.

Stop.

Just stop. Stop trying to police my feelings. Stop trying to tell me what I should think of what is going on. Stop forcing your bullshit on me. Stop giving me my own box and my own label so you don't have to think too hard about me either. So you can be comfortable like nothing is really real, like none of this is really happening.

Like you're so fucking cool, you can look down on everything. You can look down on what's real and what matters and what people really feel. You can laugh and laugh like what you pretend is so much better than reality, like you are apart from it all, way up above this pettiness.

But you are no different. Your body will betray you just the same. A car crash will drain your blood, or a cluster of damaged cells in your colon will turn cancerous, or your heart will pop in your chest while you watch reruns of Seinfeld one afternoon. The day will come. Your body will slide out of your control even though part of you was certain it would never really happen to you. You will be made small. You will be made powerless. And you will die, and we will plant you in the ground like all of the others.

And the people that care about you will be inconsolable, and other people will try to calm them down. 'Cause life goes on. And it's all part of God's plan. And they're so sorry for your loss.

And that's good enough, right?

So let's all get back to production and consumption already. There's a new show where Gordon Ramsay yells at chefs on tonight, and I want to eat a bunch of fish sticks and watch it without people crying in the background. And I want to finger fuck my smart phone all day without feeling anything real, if possible.

See?

See?

I was right, wasn't I? I should have just stayed alone. I

should have stayed away from everyone.

I should have disappeared.

"Jeff," a voice says.

I realize that I'm standing now. I see only blobs and blurs through the tears, but based on the voice I think it's Cromwell.

"What?" I say.

There's a pause. It suddenly feels very silent here. Awkward.

"Just be quiet for a minute, man," he says. "I'm sorry."

"OK," I say.

I feel embarrassment. Not so much that I care what these other people think. I feel embarrassed and vulnerable as I forgot they were even here. I forgot I was even here in a way. I got lost in my thoughts and felt alone.

So they want me to be quiet. Was I crying too loudly for their delicate sensibilities?

Wait.

I was having that hypothetical argument out loud, ranting at myself, I think. Yelling, I think.

But yeah... It's fine. It's really just as well.

Who fucking cares?

And then I'm crying all the way again. The red and hot and wet spread across my face, descending over me like a cloak of hurt that smothers me and blocks the rest of the world out. I twitch and flail. I try not to fight it, but I do. So I weep, and I strain against it involuntarily. I think the struggle makes the sobs more anguished, more frustrated.

Pain catches in my throat and tries to choke me before its music passes through my lips. This happens over and over. I feel myself sink down into the heat like I'm leaving reality and going somewhere else, a darker place, a wet place. And I have a memory of feeling this sensation before, when I was a toddler or maybe even an infant. I knew it then, what it feels like to descend into this inconsolable place, this wounded and helpless place.

And pictures open in my head of Glenn:

He pulls on the DAMN SEAGULLS trucker hat outside of the diner, his eyes a little paranoid looking as we head into our undercover work.

A black and white version of him squats in some bushes in the other world, talking to me through a mirror. He looks tired. His beard sprouts thick wires of hair, matted down in some areas and fluffed up in others.

He feeds the cats and guards the food from Leroy, his mouth stuck in a permanent half smile as he shuffles his feet to block the cat's advances repeatedly, like a blocker picking up a blitzing linebacker.

He shovels faux Australian food into his face at Outback, his mouth juicy, his eyes crazed with gluttony, his mustache sporting barbecue sauce like a loaded paintbrush.

And I am underwater now, submerged in some warm liquid that separates me from the rest of the universe. Does my body flood me in warmth like this to try to help me stop being sad? Is it supposed to comfort me? Is it trying to make me feel safe and warm?

I don't.

And I remember how I felt at the Outback with Glenn when I couldn't stay awake. I floated face down. That's how I described it then, that I floated face down through my life.

And now I am under. I am sinking. And hitting the bottom might be a relief. It really might.

I try to put my hand over my face, but it doesn't work right. I try it again, but something is wrong. It takes a second to figure it out. A piece of rope holds my wrists together. I can't get either palm flat to my face. So I just hold my two stupid hands in front of me, my thumbs leaning into my forehead like I'm praying into them instead of crying.

And voices are yelling, and I know somehow that they've been yelling for a while now. They sound far away and weird and wet like all of us really are underwater.

But I think they're yelling at me, barking commands, trying to make me do something.

Can't they see how much I don't care about any of that? I don't even remember what's going on here, exactly. Can't they see that? Can't they see I have other concerns at the moment?

I don't want to do whatever they want me to do. I don't even want to breathe.

Something thumps me on the back of the head again, but I don't mind. What difference does it make at this point, you know? I'll just take a little nap is all.

CHAPTER 33

I fall into the black again, just like I did after that black fog surrounded me in the alley. But I feel no fear this time. I do not scream. I do not wave my arms.

I hurt.

I feel the place where Glenn is supposed to be, the piece of my consciousness where he resides, and it's like something has been ripped out by the roots. Like if the dentist took pliers to your teeth. Like that, but bigger.

One person out of all of the billions that have walked the Earth, out of all of the billions of years the planet has existed. The idea that I would even meet and know that one person is so unlikely from that perspective. But I did. I knew him for part of that tiny fraction of time he existed. And he was funny and interesting and smart and an endless well of thoughts and feelings and dreams that were all his own. It was a miracle that he lived and breathed. A miracle.

And now he is gone for good. Forever.

One second he was alive, and the next he was dead. Every morning that I wake up for the rest of my life, Glenn will be dead.

And if we had just done things slightly differently, he'd still be alive, probably for many years. Just one different choice. If I had hidden instead of locking onto Farber's face. If we kept trying to talk to Amity via the sleep thing instead of cracking open the wall and taking the direct route. A million other things. Endless options we could have pursued. They would have averted this.

And he would still be alive.

The blackness is everywhere. It is everything. It is the only thing.

And that's fine.

I fall for a long time, the sinking feeling dominating me, filling me with that nausea you get when you think too hard, when you worry too hard, when you think about where every story ends, and why you're here, and why you bother to carry on, when you think about the broken pieces that can't be put back together again.

I try to remember the last thing Glenn said. He was quiet after we were in captivity. Did he even speak to me at the end there? I guess he told me not to run, but I don't even remember his words. I just remember the gist of him saying it, like it happened off screen.

Wait. I remember he looked scared and told me the weird shape in the distance was an altar. I think that was it. I think that was the last thing he said.

It doesn't seem right. No grand declaration of any kind. No goodbye. Just a random moment. A transient snippet of a conversation that would be forgotten under any other circumstances. It's too obscure of a moment to house his final words. It's not big enough.

I keep thinking I should tell him about all of this. Ask him about all of this. See what he thinks about all of this awful shit. But I can't, of course. I can't. I never can.

What a stupid world. Why would things work this way?

Something occurs to me just then. The alley appears in my imagination. My alley. I see the noose. I see the gray. I see the hooded figure creeping closer. And for the first time the parallel becomes clear to me.

I was brought to a place and killed over and over again, seemingly for no reason. That's like life, you know? We're brought into the world to be killed in a sense. We're all having this insane metaphysical experience that we don't understand, that we can never fully appreciate, and it ends abruptly and unexplained. We're all experiencing an incomprehensible miracle, the meaning of which forever eludes us.

Life is it.

Did something bring me to the alley to try to teach me that, or did my imagination reflect that into whatever energy that connects us all? You know, the thing in quantum physics Glenn talked about. The infinite energy that connects all of us and is somehow faster than the speed of light or whatever. Do my dreams transmit things to that place? Or does it transmit things to me?

Maybe it's both. Maybe it doesn't matter. That's all behind the scenes. Life is what happens on the stage.

It's part flesh, and it's part consciousness. We don't know how they fit together. Not for sure. When the flesh dies, do we die? Is Glenn – the energy, the consciousness – somewhere else now? Does he go somewhere else or does he flicker out?

I don't know.

But the life part for the flesh - that ends. It ends for everyone.

And the bottomless black nothing all around me brightens

ever so faintly. It shows what it's made of, just a little. The light comes up. The black dissolves.

And red surrounds me. The primal color. The red on the inside that spills out of us when you slice our skin. The red on the inside that we see flashes of in moments of wrath, moments of vengeance. The wet, hot red on the inside of all of us.

And I find a red purpose here in the blackest moment. I find a reason to not disappear just yet.

Because Riston Farber is red on the inside, and when I open him up, it will all drain out. He will end like all the rest.

CHAPTER 34

I bubble up to the surface slowly. My eyes pulse open and closed a few times, the sounds around me fading in and out in unison with the light and darkness.

First I see only the ground, snow-covered land. It rolls by beneath me like I'm walking, but my legs are still. I do hear the crunch of footsteps beating through the snow again, though. They're close.

I see motion out of the corner of my eyes, but it's blocked from my view, I guess by my torso? Ah, I see. My head sags down onto my chest. Pretty uncomfortable now that I think about it.

I tell my neck to lift my head. It doesn't seem to be in the mood to do that. It bobs up and back down twice before I can make the motion stick.

There. Now I see. Woods and Cromwell carry me, each with one of their arms hooked under one of mine in such a manner that there's a shoulder digging into each of my armpits.

I look around for a moment. The sky is going black. Was it real before? Is it blackening because of what they did to Glenn? Or are we just walking into a new place where it's dark out? Not sure. There's still a little light to see by for the moment, either way. It's a dusk type darkness, and the snow reflects however much light there is, so it looks quite a bit brighter still.

Black trees populate the landscape again, and they're not as sparse as they were earlier today. Branches of opposing trees cross like they froze amid sword fights. I take this to mean that we left the tundra some time ago. Even so, snow stretches as far as I can see.

I let my head loll back down. Why bother telegraphing that I'm awake? They'd only make me walk on my own if they knew. Let 'em carry me, I say. It doesn't feel so great to have collar bones grinding into that soft place under each arm, but I'll conserve some energy this way.

I watch the ground a while. I note that the snow here isn't as deep as the stuff we traversed earlier. I guess we must truly be on our way out of this winter wonderland.

So... yay.

The crunching seems to change somehow. Part of the sound shifts spatially, seems to move from behind me to the left to right next to me and then ahead. I tilt my head up just a little to see Farber stride out in front of the group now, leading the way. He's right in front of me, hood nodding and billowing a touch with each step.

Looking at him makes me want to spit. Heat crawls up over my shoulders, climbs my neck and grips my cheeks. Not the crying warmth this time. A hateful heat. Homicidal.

I watch the drapey bits of his dumbshit robe flap and waver. I watch the wobble of his upper carriage as each footstep grinds down into the snow. Something about his walk is pompous.

I take a deep breath and let the air out of my nostrils all slow. Clouds of steam coil out of my nose. It looks like I'm breathing smoke, which is more or less how it feels.

But I have to bite back my hatred. I have to push it down.

Not yet. It has to wait. I have to...

I can't take it anymore. I shoot mind bullets out of my eyes, and they rip through his hood, penetrating the back of his head, his skull exploding hard shards and pulpy bits everywhere like a cantaloupe meeting an m-80 and showering forth flesh and seeds alike. His body slumps to the ground, the shattered skull landing first, a red river splashing out onto the snow, a faint sizzling as the red melts a groove into the white, steam rising up from what's left of his head.

OK, not really.

I can see it in my mind, but it's not real. He still walks ahead of me, bouncing along.

Wouldn't that be great, though? Mind bullets. That's my dream power, I think.

Anyway, I know killing Farber won't be that easy. I know it will require patience. I'm prepared for that. I will bide my time. I will wait for the perfect moment. For now, I hold still like a sleepy spider waiting for something small and wiggly to find itself tangled in my web.

It's a matter of time. It always is.

I let my head sink all the way and close my eyes. Rest. Rest is what I need now.

CHAPTER 35

I dream that Glenn and I sit in his library, reading books. His glasses rest on the tip of his nose, his hands fold on his belly, and one of those huge war books sprawls on his lap. We don't speak, but I have a sense of relief that he's with me. I can breathe. I can let the muscles in my neck and shoulders relax. There's almost a deja vu quality to the sensation vibrating within me. Like I knew all along that he wasn't really gone. I knew it. He couldn't be. It wasn't real. Could never be real. It wasn't possible.

The universe makes sense again. The familiar order has been restored.

I have a hard time reading my book. My eyes won't take in the words, won't stay on the page. I keep wanting to look around the room, to take it all in, to keep it. The sunlight slanting into the window, making one tilted rectangle on the floor glow, the smell of the open books, like something old and important remembered, the chime of the clock, the feeling of companionship, of not being alone, the sense that we have no reason to worry, no reason to rush, like we have all of the time in the world to just sit and read. I want to keep all of it. Because this is how things are supposed to be.

CHAPTER 36

When I wake up, my back stings. I sit up from my resting place on the ground, the back half of my body numb, caked in snow. I try to stand, but it's hard when your hands are tied together, and you can't feel most of your body. The odor of pine trees lingers in the air. It smells like Pine Sol, only more real.

"He's up," a voice says. It's Woods.

"Good," Farber says from somewhere behind me. "Help him up, and let's move on."

Footsteps beat their way to me, and I'm scooped up. At this point these guys have their hands in my armpits more often than not. They're insatiable. Of course, I barely feel it this time out of numbness. I mostly just shake around and shiver and such. I can kind of tell something grips under my arms, a little pinch, but that's it. And I know I'm going up, hovering a moment, getting my dead feet under me.

I take a second to find my balance, my legs wobbling like a pair of Jello jigglers, knees buckling, again, three times. But the hands catch me, and I try again, and everything evens out a little. The ground feels solid again, like it did in the good old days, back when I was a warm blooded ape of some type that walked upright on two legs. Those were good times.

Once I'm steady on my feet, the mitts retract from my pits. I feel so used.

A weird sensation comes over me. I try to get a handle on my state of mind, but I can't find anywhere to grip. It's all sludge in my cranium from what I can tell, the consistency of soft butter. Nothing to hold onto.

I do know this much: it's not quite right in a mostly pleasant way. My brain feels half asleep, and I think the other half is numb from the cold. It ain't so bad as it might sound, though. It really takes the edge off when you chill your brain like this.

I'm almost giddy, even. Almost.

Is drunk one of the stages of grief or something? Feels like that in a way. Feels like I drank a bunch of vodka mixed with Redbull. All of this energy burns in me, but my motor skills are terrible, and my thoughts are a little slowed down, dimmer than usual. I'm very motivated in a way, but if I were back in the real world, my aspirations would be to do something like spray paint my surname on the hood of a police car. With no pants on. A modest goal, I'd say, and very much a drunken one.

Cromwell and Woods busy themselves with ropes, strapping them around their waists. There's barely any light now, so I can't tell what they're doing.

"Let's go," Farber says.

His face stays angled away from me, which is probably for the best for both of us. Looking at him brings a loathsome feeling over me, that humiliated sensation that there are no words for; the one that drives men to kill each other for some kind of honor, some kind of pride.

And I know even now, in some way, that doing so will not satisfy me, it will not fulfill me. Even with my drunk brain I know this, but it's like there's nothing else to do, you know?

There's nothing else. There's no satisfaction left to be had, no fulfillment, so I'll settle for this. Whatever it is.

As our walk begins, I glance back and see that Cromwell and Woods pull a sled. Where the hell did that come from? Has it been with us all this time?

A blanket covers its cargo. It's a big sled, too, about as long as a coffin and wider... As soon as that thought crosses my mind, I realize what it is.

"What are you doing with him?" I say.

I address Cromwell, but Farber answers me.

"Every man deserves a decent burial," he says. "We'll take him back with us."

I want to beat Farber's face in with a hammer. Just pound it until all that's left of his head is a bloody jelly. I know that on some level taking Glenn's body back is a good thing, an act of kindness for his family and whatnot. I know that. But when Farber's mouth opens, I want to close it for him. That's all.

We walk a long while, and no one talks. The snow stands less than two inches deep now, though still firm, and there are patches of exposed land here and there, frosted grass and dried-out dirt spots, all cracked and hardened by the cold. The trees grow denser and denser until we're walking in legit woods instead of a sparsely wooded field. Pines comprise the majority here, but there are plenty of those black, dead looking trees, too.

My limbs thaw out a little as I get my body moving and heart pumping, which basically means my arms and legs tingle and throb and get pricked by a few thousand of those really fat needles all over. Thankfully, my head doesn't suffer the same fate. My brain stays half frozen or whatever, that loopy, drunk feeling keeping the darkness at bay. For now.

Should I be more scared than I am? I have no sense of where they're taking me, though I have a pretty good idea that they intend to murder me in some spectacular fashion, to sacrifice me. It just doesn't seem real, even after all I've seen.

I wasn't too scared last time, and I was wrong. So yeah. I don't know what to do with this information, though. Should I try to whip myself into some frenzy? Can you fill yourself with fear with sheer willpower? And what would that accomplish?

Wait.

I'm getting an idea. I can feel it forming, can feel my mind churning out some shiny clump of new material.

Wait for it.

Wait for it.

Oh.

Yep.

Yep, that makes sense.

I should escape. That's the idea.

A sound plan.

Maybe I'm drunker than I thought if this is just occurring to me now. I don't know. Have I mentioned that I do not have a college degree? Not even close. I'm not proud.

We stop for a moment as they switch the ropes up. Farber takes his turn at pulling the sled, taking over for Cromwell. They pull ahead of us, blazing a trail. I'm thankful that the blanket lies flat, pulled taut over the top of the sled, not showing any outline or sense of silhouette.

We must be walking into warmer territory. I can't feel the difference, personally – it's still well within the boundaries of cold to me - but the snow is wetter here. Melty. My feet slosh through slushy spots as thick as split pea soup, and the exposed dirt no longer displays cracks. It forms mud pits. All soggy. I think the sky shines a little brighter now, too, though it's hard to be sure about this.

A hand grips my elbow and pulls me to a halt. I turn to see Cromwell, the gloved index finger on his opposite hand pressed to his lips to shush me without him making a sound. Now he yanks me forward, so we're still walking, just at a slower pace. Farber and Woods pull away from us, the sled dragging behind them.

Is he going to tell me something? Maybe he'll help me escape. That'd be pretty sweet.

I look at him, study his expression for a long moment, but his face shows no emotion. He stares straight ahead with some intensity like a cat watching a woodpile, waiting hours for the mouse that lives within to come out.

I trip then, stubbing my toe on a tree root and then slipping in the mud. I right myself just in time for Cromwell to club me on the back of the head again.

I flop down into the slush, eyelids fluttering, the world whirling around me, everything out of focus. Reality fades out slowly this time.

"Hold up. He's passed out again," Cromwell says.

And a few seconds later I do.

CHAPTER 37

I wake with my hands clasped in front of me, my fingers woven through each other. Did I do that in my sleep?

And then I sense that the sounds around me are different. No snow. No more white blanket dampening everything, rolling off most of the high frequencies, softening and smoothing everything out. That's over. All of the world's bright and harsh and hard noises have been restored to their full glory.

Bony shoulders dig into my ribs once more, and the ground slides by below my dangling feet. They carry me. Again. Walking. Carrying. Knocked out. Revived. Snow to slush to grass. It feels like all of this has been going on for years. Forever.

It's brighter now. The light shines on the branches and pine boughs above us, casting a spiderweb of shadows onto the forest floor. There's still a touch of gray to the illumination. It looks like the morning, though I guess that doesn't really exist here.

So how did my unconsciousness happen upon me this time? I think back on it. Right. Cromwell bashed my skull again. What'd he do that for? Just felt like carrying me some more? All he had to do was ask. I thought we had the kind of captive – captor relationship where I didn't need to tell him that out loud. Communication issue, I guess. That's the only real problem in any relationship, isn't it?

Pine needles carpet the ground here, dried-out and orange. They pile on top of each other, matted up, extinguishing most of the foliage. Little clouds of gray billow up from beneath the orange layer every time Cromwell's feet make contact with it. This landscape proves much drier than my last stop.

My nose itches, so I bring my hands to my face and unknit my fingers to scratch it.

Ah. As soon as my hands detach from each other, the lash around my wrists almost falls off. It's very, very loose. I could pull my hands free of the rope if I wanted, though I will wait for the right moment. I'm smooth like that.

That must be what Cromwell was doing. Making an opportunity to loosen my bonds. I suppose braining me with a blunt object was probably the most fun and efficient way for him to do that. He couldn't slip me a sweet dagger on the sly or something less violent? Has this guy never heard of the old piss break as a diversion trick?

No, no. Apparently, his idea of being discrete is dishing out concussions. Blunt force trauma. Subtle.

Whatever. I shouldn't complain. In all fairness to Cromwell, I have a pretty thick skull, and I barely use my brain as it is. Both of these facts are well established, well understood. He knew what he was doing.

So now I wait. I look for my chance. I position myself to make my move.

I wiggle some, pretending like I'm just now waking up, and the men stop and set my feet on the ground. I figure I can't escape if they're toting me around, right? I've got to create some distance. I've got to walk on my own.

"If it happens again, you'll ride in the sled," Farber says.

No thanks. I'm happy to walk now, dickface.

We pick our way through the woods. More of the pines give way to oaks, maples and birches, and the pine needle flooring recedes with grasses and green leafy stuff stepping forward to fill the void. This is good. Much less visibility. Much better cover. Both excellent characteristics for those of us plotting a daring escape.

Now I'm antsy. I don't want to launch my escape pod too hastily as I may only get this one opportunity to get away. On the other hand, for all I know, our intended destination lies around the next corner. Farber might have the plastic sheets all laid out and ready to go in a serial killer style kill room just past that Douglas fir up there. So yeah. There's a real risk of waiting too long and screwing myself that way, too.

Decisions, decisions.

Of course, part of me wants to attack Farber now that I have the free hands to do it. I strangled him once. I could do it again. He wouldn't see it coming. That's for sure.

It'd be 3 on 1 most likely, though. Even if Cromwell harbors some sympathy for me, I don't see him jumping in to help me kill one or both of his friends. Seems unlikely. Maybe if I told him he'd get to hit someone over the head, he'd get so excited he wouldn't think about it too hard, but I doubt this. He could side with them and get another free shot at my skull that way. That's like the best of both worlds from his point of view.

Damn.

What should I do?

Think, Grobnagger, think!

We find a trail cutting through what is now incredibly thick vegetation and take it. Even on the path, branches grasp at my head and shake their tiny fists. Blades of various grasses smear their bodies against my jeans.

Worst lap dance ever.

We move in single file now, Farber leading the way with Woods right behind him, straining to drag the sled by himself at this point. I'm up third. I lag a little, dropping further and further back from the leaders to give myself extra distance from them. This is probably the perfect setup, the perfect chance to go for it. With Cromwell behind me, he'd be the first to see me veer off of the path, which could help me buy a little time.

I see it taking shape before it arrives, and the adrenalin courses all through me. Farber rounds a bend, moves out of view. Woods disappears into the wall of greenness as well, the sled trailing.

My heart pounds in my chest, blood thrumming in my ears, pulsing in my temples, my jaw clenched all tight.

Is this it? Should I do it?

Suddenly an arm loops through mine, hooking my left elbow and pulling me off the trail. I'm confused, being dragged through leaves and limbs and stems and stalks. A hooded figure pulls me along, zigging and zagging to avoid trees. Is Cromwell making a break for it with me?

No. This hood, while black, seems to have a red shimmer to it somehow. This person's frame occupies less space, too. Narrow shoulders. Slender waist. Much shorter.

We hit a little clearing, a straightaway through knee high grass, and she turns and smiles at me.

"Ain't no party like a rescue party," she says.

It's Amity.

CHAPTER 38

I shake my hands loose from the rope, though Amity still drags me along by the wrist. The forest remains a green blur around us. She's quite nimble, this one. She changes direction like a puma. I don't think I've ever seen a puma change directions, actually, but I bet they do so with a lot of class and style. Either way, she is very light on her feet. She moves like a ninja, all quiet and shit. I, on the other hand, crash through the woods, gigantic yeti feet tromping down ferns like the guy in the Godzilla suit destroying a miniature city.

I want to ask her about 50 questions, but it's difficult to do so while sprinting and puma leaping and gasping for breath and all. I suppose some of my queries could perhaps be unwise to speak aloud at the moment, too.

I mean, does she know? Does she know about Glenn? And should I tell her while we're in getaway mode? Probably not, right? It wouldn't help anything that I can think of.

And Glenn flashes in my head again, lifting his navy blue ball cap with his left hand and slicking his hair back with his right, splayed fingers working like giant teeth on a comb. He blinks and looks far away and pulls the cap back on.

No. Don't think about that now. Run.

I smash plants flat. I trample them. I squash them. I'll admit it. I can be a little rough with the plant life.

I hear running water now. The words, "a babbling brook," pop into my head, because my head is weird. Anyway, the water must be pretty close to be loud enough to hear over my yeti stomps. We run a while longer, take a hard right around a weeping willow, and the rushing stream appears before us, gashing a spurt of wet movement over a brown river bed that parts the green ground covering all around it.

Yep, the babbling brook itself.

We turn right again, running alongside the water. Maybe there is some biological response to seeing fresh water like this, but I think I feel better. Invigorated. Refreshed. The tension in my neck seems to dissipate. The fire in my lungs dies down to a smolder. The stabbing pain that feels like a knitting needle piercing my liver disappears entirely. Sure, I still half expect Farber to come round house kicking out from some bushes at any second, but I feel better about it.

The water smells fresh. This whole section of the woods smells alive. Awake.

Wait. I'm not great with directions necessarily, but I think we might be headed back in the direction we came from. Is that possible? I remember two pretty hard right turns. I guess that would do it, eh? Would be pretty ridiculous to run right into the dudes chasing us, right?

I tug on Amity's hand, doing the double jerk that is the universal hand language for pull over. But she's not having any of it. She yanks my arm a little harder and continues running, weaving, ninja-ing. Not so much as a glance my way.

So I keep up the best I can. Not because I'm ashamed that this girl is a superior athlete to me or anything like that. I do it because if I don't, I'm pretty sure she will rip my arm off.

Red on the Inside

The sound of the water gets louder and louder. The pitch seems lower, too, almost thunderous in the distance. The stream looks a little wider, for sure, perhaps a little deeper as well, but it must get really huge somewhere up ahead based on what I'm hearing.

Now we slalom through a cluster of sumac trees, young ones with trunks about the girth of cigars. They're packed together tightly. I try to take diagonal steps and contort my torso to avoid contact as much as possible, but it's not a huge help. Sticks scrape against me with each step. It's like running through a gauntlet that should be part of some TV game show. Each step seems to bring a new injury with it, thankfully minor. This step jabs my knee. That step rubs a patch of skin off of my forehead about the size of a quarter.

And my eyes water. And my mouth is all dry. And my throat burns, probably because the fire in my lungs packs a pretty good rage at this point.

The water is a never ending crash of thunder now, and I realize that there must be a waterfall up ahead, a pretty big one by the sounds of it. That suggests a cliff, which consequently suggests a possible detour ahead for us.

This is all too complicated for my liking. Couldn't we just find a nice spot to lie down, shrouded in all the cover the green supplies? That'd be cool. And how would they find us, honestly? These woods stretch out forever. They can't turn over every leaf or poke through every bush. They could search for days and never get within 150 feet of us.

You know what? Yeah. I vote for that. Let's lie down ASAP.

I consider how to broach this topic with Amity, especially without using words since I'm too busy trying to breathe to speak right now.

But just then her hand disengages from mine, and she turns to me and lips something at me, but I can't hear her. Then she splashes out into the stream and jumps over the edge of the waterfall where the river drops off into nothing.

CHAPTER 39

I stand on the bank of the river, too scared to even get close enough to the edge to peek over the falls. The loudness of crashing water vibrates the world. I feel it through my feet and rattling in my ribcage. Mist kicks up into the air all around here, a little spritzing my forehead, cooling me. So that's nice, at least.

Nothing is ever just simple, right? Remember my idea about lying down in the weeds? Now, what the hell was wrong with that? But no, no, let's hurl ourselves over a damn waterfall instead.

I think people underestimate how frustrating it can be to realize that pretty much everyone is more brave than you.

So what am I supposed to do? I can feel my eyebrows twitch as my brain works this out. My mouth hangs open, my lungs rapid fire huffing and puffing to try to get some wind in me.

I was pretty taken aback by this waterfall leap, right? Right. OK. Just making sure.

I run it back. She turned to me just before she leapt off the edge of the world. She turned to me, and her mouth moved. She spoke one syllable, but I couldn't hear her over the roar of the water rushing over the falls. Did she whisper? Did she yell? I suppose it makes no difference. But I can still see her lips opening at the beginning of the word and then pushing together at the end. It ended with a p, I believe.

I watch her lip the word at me in my imagination over and over, and I try to read it. Ah, OK, it ends with an "mp" now that I think about it. By process of elimination, I believe I can narrow this down to "jump" or "hump."

Now, for me personally, it'd be a lot funnier if she turned and yelled "hump" at me just before plummeting off of these falls. I would like that quite a bit. Plus, she could be making plans for what we're going to do later. Also awesome.

But no, she was telling me to jump, I guess. Damn it. Everybody just assumes I'm like Indiana Jones or Tom Brady or something, but I am more like Marcia Brady.

My feet pad over the muddy banks, walking all slowly because part of me, maybe most of me, never actually wants to arrive at the edge and look down. I manage to really stretch this mosey out, kicking at pebbles, taking in all of the sights and sounds on the 20 foot route. I even strike up a small talk conversation with myself:

Boy, it's a nice day isn't it? The warm air, the sound of the falls, that little touch of mist in the air. Oh man, I'm telling you, a guy could get used to this. He could get used to it real quick.

But I don't feel like myself. It all comes off like I'm pretending, going through the motions of being alive. I haven't felt like myself since Glenn's death, I guess. Like the best I can do is disconnect from what's going on, detach from my surroundings, my reality. Things can seem funny again when I'm far away from it, when nothing is real. Is that the best it can ever be? Ironic detachment? Floating above the world with a layer of absurdity swathing everything.

I don't know. I may never feel like myself again.

I look over the edge, my toes nearing the point at which the ground shears off into a cliff wall at about a 90 degree angle. It's about 30 feet down, I'd say. A pile of jagged rock chunks occupy the place directly beneath me. It looks like the spot straight down from the falls is the place to jump. There's a rounded area there just beyond the splash zone where the water is fairly still. I assume it's deeper than the rest.

I don't see Amity, though. Maybe she took cover in the woods.

Well, I guess I should go for it. You only live once. Or twice, I guess, if you resurrect after an old man burns you alive in the bottom of a well. (Is that a thing that happens to people, or was it just something that happened to me the one time?)

I wade out into the wetness. It's a little over knee deep where I stand, but the river grows more shallow going toward the falls. The stream widens as it gets to the drop off, the water pulled thin as it passes over the rock corner and dumps off the edge.

I take a deep breath and let it out all slow. I never do shit like this. My fear is too big, always has been. Even as a kid, while everyone else possessed this false sense of immortality, I feared injury and death all of the time. I was the kid that couldn't make a tackle in football with my eyes open, didn't want to jump off of the roof onto the trampoline to see what happened, didn't think it was fun to get the 4 wheeler going full speed. I'm that tiny percent of scaredy cats that must be necessary to ensure that the entire species doesn't get wiped out by head trauma or eating poison mushrooms.

Another deep breath, the exhale flowing out of me, deflating my ribcage. The water refuses me a moment of silent reflection. It roars and crashes into the rocks and generally taunts me.

I close my eyes and block everything out for a moment. I picture myself soaring over the edge, long jumping like an Olympian, legs churning in the empty air, face all stoic like I've done this a million times before. Something about it is like a silent film.

I can do this. I have nothing to lose and all to gain. It's a leap of faith, or a leap to faith, as Randy said shortly before he covered me in gas and set me on fire.

See? I've made it through worse.

I open my eyes. The watery sounds fade back into my consciousness.

I run ten paces, my speed building as the water gets shallower and shallower. The edge comes up on me. I gulp in one last breath, hold it.

And jump.

CHAPTER 40

The bottom of the world drops out, and I fall into nothing, into empty space. Everything flicks into slow motion. My arms flail one time a piece in something akin to a swim move that I believe is some kind of recoil or follow through from the exertion of the lift-off jump itself. I seem to float at first, just ever so faintly dropping and without much velocity. Like I might just be able to do one of those astronaut jumps and nestle into a touchdown on the opposite shore.

That half nauseous, half exhilarated feeling bubbles in my stomach as the fall continues. It feels me sinking before it really happens, tries to brace me for it.

From there, the angle of my motion bends quickly to straight down. My descent picks up speed at an ever increasing rate. The air rushes against me, tears pooling in my eyes and draining from the corners.

Good news: I'm headed right for the deeper pool of water. Knowing I won't get chewed up by that mouth of jagged stones makes me feel a little better. I'll probably just hit my head and drown in this calm pool, which should be a much less painful way to go.

Good deal.

I don't churn my legs like I did when I imagined this jump. In fact, I straighten out a little more than I would like, feet pointed down. This isn't great. I think if you hit the water feet first with your knees locked, you can hyperextend that shit pretty badly, maybe even tear some ligaments. I try to not lock them, but it's hard to concentrate on things like this while also focusing on not pissing and shitting yourself in terror.

Falling faster and faster and I hit the water with a slapping sound and keep going, submerged, the shock of cold hugging against me, its embrace broken up only by the air bubbles rocketing past on all sides. And the sound cuts off as the water surrounds me, muted, deadened. Not silent – I can hear a muffled version of the waterfall that reminds me more of stampeding elephants now – but mostly sounds are turned inward. I hear my heart beat louder, and the sounds of swallowing saliva magnified. And I keep my eyes open during all of this, which surprises me. I'm more of a flincher, or I was, at least. I always was.

Momentum carries me down and down into the deep, the chill growing more intense as I go. The cold grips my torso in a way that makes it hard to breathe, like it's too chilly and my lungs just want to quit now and get it over with.

Looking up I can see the light illuminating those top layers of water, shimmering in the choppiness, an expanding ring of ripples my splash landing created. I can see where I need to go, maybe 15 feet up or so, but I'm powerless to get there, still going down, slower than before, but it's too much force to fight still.

But I can't panic either. I can't. If I waste energy fighting the momentum of the fall, I'll be much worse off. So I stay patient. I wait.

The sinking slows to almost nothing, a drift that's as much

sideways as descending. When my downward motion reaches its end, I hover there a second as the forces that pull me down and up negotiate their equilibrium. Then the weight lifts off of me, and a great lightness takes its place. I float upward just a touch, and I know it's time. I kick my legs and reach out with cupped hands now to help floating along.

Even with the kicks, rising to the surface takes longer than I'd like. I almost wish I had gotten to the sandy bottom so I'd have something to push off of. The light gets brighter. The surface grows nearer and nearer, but some part of me panics anyway. It remains convinced that I'll never get there, that I'll never bob up through the top, move back into the light, and draw fresh air into my lungs. It remains convinced that the liquid will hold me under in some suffocating hug, its arms surrounding me forever.

I breach the threshold, pushing face first through the surface and feeling the open air again. It's almost shocking for that roaring waterfall sound to click back on, to feel the air that seems to stretch out into the sky like it never ends, to be bombarded with daylight. I blink twice, and my lungs creak and hiss as the first breath gasps into me. Breath number two gets interrupted by a mouthful of water, which I thankfully catch and spit out right away rather than inhale. I taste a little sulfur in there, I think.

Yum.

I want this to be over. I want to swim to the shore and be on the land. But I tread water for a moment, trying to get my wind back before I make the swim out.

Patience. Maybe I am learning something. Maybe I am changing.

Maybe I will never feel like myself again because my self isn't some static thing. It changes with everything I do, every experience, every conversation. It rolls in and out like the tide, every wave unique. When I think about it that way, I don't feel quite as bad. It hurts me a lot, and I might never get over it, I might never heal, but at least I can say that Glenn taught me a lot of shit. He changed me for the better. That's something, right?

I swim to the shore and crawl up the mud that slopes along the bank to lie in the grass, rolling over onto my back and closing my eyes. My breath heaves in and out of me, and I shiver a little, though I'm somehow too hot and too cold at the same time. Clammy all over. I open my eyes and look up at the treetops, at the barrier of cloud hung above them.

And Glenn pops into my head, wielding a plate of jerked chicken with that cheesy rice and bean concoction. And then he's walking through his backyard, arms limp at his sides, his posture somehow like an overgrown toddler's.

There was nothing I could do, but I should have done something, you know? I should have done something. I should have. There was nothing I could do, but I should have done it anyway.

And my face clenches up, those balls of muscle hardening at the crook on each side of my jaw, and I know I was wrong. That shit I thought before about Glenn changing me? It didn't make this any better. Nothing makes it any better. Nothing makes it make any sense.

I burst into tears again. They rush down my face, and my chest spasms, and my body squirms on the grass without me telling it to, and strange noises rattle out of me that don't sound

216

like me, and I know in my heart that nothing will ever make it better.

CHAPTER 41

When Amity finds me, I am under that blanket of wet, hot red again, plunging into the gloom inside of me, blocking out reality. I don't fully realize she is there at first.

I gurgle up to the surface, poking my head out of the internal world into a moment of clarity, seeing her silhouette, a dark shape against the light. I know what I need to do now, and it will hurt some more. For both of us.

Amity kneels on the line at the edge of the stream where the dirt gives way to grass. I swallow, and it's loud – a gulp and a click. I half sit up and rub my hand against my chest like I'm smoothing out some wrinkles before my big speech. I take a beat, our eyes locked. I wanted to gather myself, and I think I've done an OK job. I know how much worse this will be for her than it is for me, which is hard to fathom, but I know it's true.

I muster some gravitas. I don't know why, but it seems necessary.

But as I speak that flash of heat comes over me again. I sink into the darkness, the emptiness. I know the words are coming out of my mouth. I know from the outside it probably seems fine – the gravity is right, the empathy is right. But I am disconnected from it, plummeting deeper inside myself. It's like someone else does the talking, someone stronger than I am.

Red on the Inside

I tell her about the snow and the rope and the swords. All of it. And I ultimately succeed at dragging her down here with me, engulfing her in the sorrow and anger and powerlessness.

And we lie on the grass for a long time, and we rip our insides out and let the air touch them and let the mist touch them. We pour out our souls through our mouths and eyes without saying a word.

And the water just keeps thundering over the edge and clobbering the rocks below, totally indifferent.

CHAPTER 42

At some point I realize that we've just been lying still for a long time, and I think about how Farber is surely looking for us. It hadn't even crossed my mind in a long while.

I sit up. It's been so quiet that I almost expect to find Amity asleep. She is awake. She stares up into the heavens, a dead expression in her eyes. Redness still splotches her cheeks. Moisture still shines on the swollen eyelids.

"We should get moving, right?" I say, my voice sounding deeper than normal like I just woke up. "You know they're still looking for me."

She doesn't blink. The dead expression doesn't change at all, in fact.

"They won't find us," she says. "But we should get going anyway."

I pinch that place where my nose connects to my forehead and lift. I don't know why. I saw a guy doing it at a restaurant once, and I tried it. Seems to relieve some tension. Maybe it's some kind of pressure point or something.

"How do you know they won't find us?" I say.

She sits up, brushing away the dirt that clings to the backs of her arms.

"I know these woods a lot better than they do," she says. "Unless they decide to jump off the falls like we did, they'll never find us. They won't find an easier way down here. It doesn't exist."

I nod.

"Well, that's good," I say, though I consider saying, "clever girl," like that scene in Jurassic Park where the guy gets eaten by velociraptors. Probably should have gone with that. Damn.

I lift myself to one knee and stretch my back, arching my neck and rotating my core a little. My muscles fight this movement, wanting to remain rigid and motionless, but I won't allow such nonsense. I stretch them harder, putting some stank on it. They shouldn't have challenged me. I can be pretty coldblooded with this kind of stuff, pretty callous.

I stand. My calves give me a little pinch once my full weight rests on them. They are sore to a degree that I never really expected to experience here. Kind of weird. I bounce up and down on my toes a few times to try to limber those babies up.

Amity stands and rolls her neck a few times, scrunches her shoulders. She is so much shorter than me that it's hard to believe we are members of the same species. It must be about a foot and a half difference. The top of her head comes up to my nipples.

She mops at her top lip with the back of her tiny hand as if on cue to illustrate my point. She has those cute, little elf ears, too. Maybe that is her species: elf.

I believe we've already established that my species is troll, or maybe I'm some hybrid of troll and yeti. I could buy that.

Without saying anything, she walks into the woods. I follow. The plant life seems a touch more suffocating down here. Prickly stuff grabs at my shirt. Branches snap off of Amity, threatening me by shaking leaves in my face, almost daring me to take another step. The green smothers me. It grinds itself on me.

And then we hit a clear spot, and that's all over. We now trot on a reasonably well worn path, heading deeper into the woods where the shade gets thicker. The canopy above knits its leaves together tightly so only pinpoints of light ripple through when the air moves. It's like we're walking into the dusk.

The roar of the waterfall trails off into nothing as we move along.

"So where are we going?" I say.

"I know a place we can hide out for a while," she says. "There are a couple of apple trees, and a spring where the water doesn't have that sulfur taste."

"Do you need food out here?" I say.

"Not much," she says. "I think getting some water to drink once in a while helps keep your mind clear, though, and the apples always make me feel better."

"So a comfort thing more than a nutrition thing?" I say.

"Yeah, exactly," she says. "Anyway, we should be safe to stay there as long as we want. I figure if we wait long enough, they'll be gone, and we can get back to wandering around. Time is hard to judge out here, but Farber and his people don't seem to stay more than a couple days at a time or something that feels like that. Not sure what that translates to in the real world, but I think it's like 40 days or so."

I look down at myself as my brain digests her words. My feet kick up dust with every step, not clouds so much as puffs of gray that resettle on the ground as quickly as they appear.

"So you were planning for me to stay here a while?" I say. "Cause I was kind of figuring to get back as soon as possible."

"What for?" she says. "Farber is trying to kill you, right? You stick with me, and that will never happen. Not a chance he'll find us. It's peaceful out here, you know? There's a lot of interesting stuff to do. Lots of things I could show you."

"I don't know. There are matters back there that I need to take care of," I say.

"Well, it's your choice," she says. "But there's nothing back there that you'd miss. You know that, don't you?"

I think it over.

"I don't know if that's true," I say. "I mean, don't you want to go to your Dad's funeral or whatever?"

She stops walking, blinks a few times. When she starts going again, her gaze shifts to the ground. We walk in silence for a while, moving past sections of woods that are difficult to distinguish from the rest. The green is so dense above us and so sparse on the ground. The lack of light coming through leads to mostly dead leaves and barren trunks down here. There are a few ferns that must like the shade here and there, but that's it.

I'm glad to have this path to tell us where to go. Elsewise the woods grow intimidating as we walk in their shadows. Indecipherable. Claustrophobic. I feel a little lost, even though I know Amity knows it all inside and out.

She speaks again, and after the distractions, it takes me a second to catch up with the conversation.

"I can't go back," she says. "I don't make sense there anymore."

CHAPTER 43

The trees thin out in time and let some spots of light sift between the leaves and branches. My dread recedes as we move out of the shade, into the warmth. Daylight melts anxiety, I think, at least somewhat.

I watch Amity as we walk. Her body language is foreign to me: upright posture with a sense of power or athleticism in that section of the torso where the abs meet the ribcage. There's a bounce in her step, a sureness even in the way her arms go back and forth at her sides. She moves with a confidence that I'll never have. Not cockiness. Not arrogance. It's not something for show. It's no attempt to intimidate. It's genuine. You can see it.

Even her build exudes confidence. She is not one of those waif girls with little toothpick arms, nor does she look like a bodybuilder or anything like that. Her physique remains feminine. There's something strong about her, though. A toughness. An anger that flashes in her eyes sometimes and tenses up in her shoulders at others.

Am I saying that she seems like a tough elf? Yeah, I guess I am. She's about as tough as a girl that's about five feet tall can be, at least.

In any case, as a bona fide sissy, this assertive personality type always makes me uneasy. Like maybe I will say or do something wrong, and she will lash out or judge me harshly. Look, it's a matter of time before she turns on me. I've been around. I know this.

The path coils around a couple of bends, and the trees alongside us fall away. A grass field opens up ahead of us. It looks familiar. It looks a lot like that too-perfect grass field that led me to the tree. This field displays some imperfections, though – a few taller stalks gone to seed sprout here and there. They rasp when the wind blows.

That comprises another difference itself. The wind seems more legit here. It gusts and dies out just like the real thing. There was something very artificial about it on the way to the tree. More like breath than wind, or maybe more like a machine, even.

Still, the grassy expanse before us bears a strong resemblance to the other one. Maybe this is the way there? That question postures on the tip of my tongue, ready to dive out of my mouth. I push the urge down, though. Some part of me doesn't want to break up the silence yet.

It's neither an unpleasant silence nor an all the way comfortable one, but something about it feels right just now, so I leave it alone. Amity makes eye contact with me for a second, her eyes scanning back and forth across my face with a questioning look. I get a little nervous about what she might see. Just a little. Then, apparently finding some kind of answer there, she smiles at me, and I smile at her. We go back to looking at other things and maintaining the quiet.

See? It's nice to have a silent friend like this.

Blades of green swish against our pant legs as we move into the taller grass. It feels so strange to walk out into the open, no longer hidden amongst the trees. I look out to the horizon now rather than being encased in green leaves. The land just flattens out like it lied down here to nap for a bit and forgot to wake up. There's something satisfying about being able to see what's going on around you, even if I also get that twinge of vulnerability that comes with being exposed.

The air here must be warmer as it's not long before I feel the sweat collecting on my forehead, briny fluid draining from the corners of my brow. I wipe the back of my neck, not surprised to find more moisture. That sensation proves shocking in its own way. Not long ago, I trudged through knee deep snow, shivering. I woke up like a popsicle, caked in white powder, numb as could be from upper back to lower sack. Now I'm all greased up with perspiration.

It's a small astral plane after all.

We walk, grass all we can see in any direction. For a while, I could look back at the tree line to gauge how far we'd come, but the horizon swallowed that up some time ago. Now? Only grass. The wind gusts in our faces every so often, and the air feels cool as it glides across my skin. Something about it is just enough to keep this trek over a monotone green from becoming tedious.

"It's not far now," Amity says, squinting at me.

These are the first words spoken between us for what feels like days. Her voice sounds a little tired, just a touch of gravel to it, but it's nice. You forget how stimulating a human voice can be until the sound leaves you for a while. When it comes back, it makes your heart beat faster. It makes your eyelids flutter. It makes a tingle spread down your arms and throb in the palms of your hands.

I think about this before I answer her, though. Because maybe that's not true of all voices. Maybe it's true of her voice in particular. But I push the thought aside.

"You mean the place with the apple trees," I say.

She clears her throat. It's weird. When I do that, it sounds like some grotesque troll mating call, like tectonic plates of phlegm vibrate in my throat in such a manner that trolls happen to find arousing. When she does it, it sounds so small. Dainty. Trolls wouldn't find it stimulating, I think. They would just go, "Awww."

"No," she says. "You said you want to go back, so we're going to the tree."

"Oh, right," I say.

So I guess this grass field does lead to the other one. Good to know. But wait.

"So are you coming with me?" I say.

She shakes her head.

"I don't think so," she says. She looks far away for a second, and then she smiles. "I think I'm walking you home."

CHAPTER 44

The tree seems to take shape out of the mist all at once, its size still hard to believe even though I've seen the thing before. It remained invisible until we were quite close this time. After giving this some thought, I decide we're approaching it from a different direction, thereby changing the appearance of things pretty dramatically as it turns out. So it goes.

The mist douses us, though, just like before. So that hasn't changed a bit. The clots of moisture hang in the air, tiny droplets all over the damn place. We have no choice but to walk through them. We do that. I'm typically not a fan of sogginess, but this doesn't feel too bad. I was too warm much of the way, so it's kind of a relief.

Amity carries her robe, draping it over her arm. The fabric sways, and it glimmers when the light hits it right. Pretty fancy shit.

Her hair is a bit shorter than I realized now that it's out in the light and I can really see it. She wears a black tank top, visible with the robe removed. I try not to ogle her too much, but I am a disgusting troll, so what do you expect? Anyway, I have gotten the strong impression that I'm not her type, so it's not like that. I don't take as much joy in eyeballing girls that aren't into me, you know? I mean, I do it involuntarily and compulsively, but I don't enjoy it as much.

Sigh.

Not that she has been mean to me or anything like that. She's really nice, and I get it. I'm not my type, either. You know how those jerk-offs have those decals that say, "No Fat Chicks," on the rear windshields of their shitty cars? They should make those that say, "No Disgusting Trolls," so I'd know who not to approach. I can't speak for the other trolls, but I wouldn't be offended by that.

Anyway.

The tree's trunk takes up much of my frame of vision now. Pretty big. The clusters of roots jut out of the ground around us, but they're neither as big nor as plentiful as they were in the place where I met up with Glenn.

Shit. Don't think about him. Not now. There will be time later. Fight it, Grobnagger. Change the subject, right? Right. So, um...

"So what's with the tree?" I say.

"What do you mean?" she says.

"I don't know," I say. "Why does it... do the thing it does?"

She shrugs, cupped hands facing the sky.

"Well, um... What kind of question is that, really? I mean, why does anything exist?" she says.

I wait for her to go on. She doesn't. Is it just me, or do her and her dad get a lot of mileage out of rhetorical questions? I guess that quality can run in families.

"Why does anything exist?" I repeat back to her. "I don't know."

"Exactly," she says. "I don't know if there's a reason why the tree does anything, or a reason why this place is here, or why we're here. I figure in all likelihood, I'll never know these

229

things, not the why part anyway."

"Doesn't that seem shitty, though?" I say.

"In a way," she says. "But I don't worry much about it. I am finding out how things work or at least fragments of that, and that is interesting enough for me. For all I know, there is no reason why, and that's OK."

We walk, and I think it over. I don't like it, but I don't say anything. I mean, she could be right, but I don't like it. I want to know why some day, not just how. It might be impossible, but I want it anyway.

"Nobody knows what they're doing," she says. "We all just make it up as we go, fashioning the pieces of information that we have into a reality. It's all a little bit make believe, you know?"

I don't know what to say. There is a fatalism to this girl that I love and hate. These words sound, to some degree, like something I might say, and even so, hearing someone else say them is painful in some way. I want to tell her that you can't let those things in, that you have to bludgeon these thoughts and keep them outside of you. But I say nothing.

The grass grows patchy underfoot, receding to dust. The tree stands within 200 yards now. We could sprint to it and be there within a few seconds, but I believe we will walk. As you may know, I'm no fan of unnecessary exertion.

But my mind flips into record mode again, like I know this chapter is ending, and as awful as it was, I feel weird about leaving it. The ache of vulnerability creeps upon me as I prepare to change settings, perhaps more so than ever. And who can I even trust now? Who can I talk to?

I picture Glenn doing that move where it looked like he was

clawing at his mustache, and tears come into my eyes. I mostly fight them back, but Amity turns to me right then, lips flattened against each other as she studies my expression again.

"You sure you don't want to just stay here?" she says.

"There's something I have to do," I say. "Maybe a couple of things."

She looks up at the tree.

"I understand," she says.

A new kind of quiet falls over us. I don't know what to make of it, but it's tense in a way that makes our feet scuffing in the dust sound really loud. Self consciousness takes hold in a way that makes breathing suddenly seem strange. I try to remember how to do it comfortably. My first attempts come out too shallow, almost panting, and then I overcompensate and do it too slow and deep.

"Well, make me a promise?" she says.

Before I can react, she pounces on me in a hug that pins my arms to my sides. I wriggle to get free enough to hug her back.

"What's that?" I say.

She leans back to look up at me.

"Promise me you'll come back," she says.

I nod.

"I promise," I say.

She stands on her tiptoes and closes her eyes to kiss me then. I stoop a little to make it work. Just a peck on the lips. I don't even know what to make of it. But I still feel the tingle on my lips and only that when I stumble along in a daze and touch the tree and everything disappears.

CHAPTER 45

A sandy brick facade masks the front of the building, and elegant gold lettering sparkles like this is some fancy bed and breakfast. It's not.

Pushing through the steel door, red carpet runs down the narrow hallway, and the cinder block walls are painted white. It's chilly here, and just looking at those concrete walls somehow makes it feel even colder. The florescent lighting yellows everything a little. Like a dead tooth.

Arrangements of flowers sit on every table, stand, ledge and any other flat surface. Some even arrive in standing baskets mounted on their own metal legs. The little clusters of mostly muted rainbows line the hall. Each a little different and all exactly the same. The odor of lilies, snapdragons, mums, roses, poms and all the others shift and congeal in the air. Every breath gulps in the smorgasbord of a perfume that is totally natural and somehow vaguely unpleasant.

The way vomit smells too sweet.

Turning right through the red velvet curtain and into the main chamber, the flowers now pile high to the left and right of the room's centerpiece along the front wall. Crammed, wedged and squeezed onto shelves, the baskets and ceramic pots jockey for position. Flowers floor to ceiling, and they just keep coming.

Red on the Inside

They flood the shelves, and the overflow splashes down onto the carpet. Waves of white lilies flow across the floor, crashing up against potted yellow roses and a sympathy cross made of white orchids with a border of deep green palms. A white gardenia topiary sinks between a couple of wreaths in stands. A pink everlasting love wreath made of roses and hydrangeas spills out into the aisle. Now even more flowers lurch onto the main floor, hug the wall farther out still, stretch for the doorway. More and more and more.

The plants seep slowly toward the rows of folding chairs, desperately reaching their stems out away from death.

CHAPTER 46

Why are you here?

You detach until it isn't even real. You're aware it's happening, but all true meaning has been removed. You watch it transpiring, and your mind records the sounds and images, but the feelings have all numbed away. The connection is bad somehow. Broken.

The casket sits in the front of the room like a big black Cadillac. The hood is closed, but what a beauty. A finely crafted product. All smooth and shiny. Sleek. The lines curve just right. You can picture it having a leather interior and pop-up nav screens. Dual zone climate control. Maybe even those Xenon headlamps that shine blue. Power everything. This is the Eddie Bauer edition of coffins. The Titan series. Top of the line. It beams luxury, comfort, and style, but you're not quite sure who the beneficiary is.

Sunlight glints through stained glass windows, casting red and blue and yellow streaks that stretch across the floor, painting stripes of color on the coffin. People walk by, paying their respects to the family, hugging, shaking hands, blue light smearing their faces.

The chatter permeating the room maintains a hush, a reverence.

Why are you here? You don't do this. You don't go to

funerals. You don't go to hospitals. You don't go out to eat or answer social calls of any kind. That is who you are. And the abortion unfolding in this room is why.

Because you saw what really happened. You saw the body slumped face down, blood seeping from a menagerie of holes. You saw this. You saw it.

Everything between you and Glenn ended there, didn't it? So who is this for?

Why are you here?

CHAPTER 47

And now the people huddle around the box, and the man in black speaks, and he points his finger in the book, and he points his pig nose at the book, and his voice quivers with veneration and quavers with deference, but his words ring vague, ring hollow, ring out the emptiness like a bottomless hole of black nothing in ourselves, in our culture, in our souls that can never be filled, cause this is the same goddamn shit he reads for all of them, for all of the heart attack victims or cancer dads or guys that got hit by a drunk driver or whatever, like if he sells it well enough with a shaky voice and puppy dog eyes it'll really mean something, like it's not some empty gesture, like this isn't just another assembly line pumping out their, "Hallmark card speech for a guy who died fairly young," product so everyone can try to feel OK about it, and the people stay huddled around the box, and they bow their heads and bob their heads and sigh their stupid fucking heads off at all of the appropriate moments, and they're sorry, sorry, so sorry for your loss, like whoops, sorry about that, my bad, y'all, like they just took out your blue piece in the board game "Sorry!" or some shit, and the people huddle around the box and clap each other on the shoulder and pat each other on the back and offer each other Kleenex to dab their stupid fucking eyes out with, and the man in black finishes up his routine, and he lifts his pig nose out of the book and shuts it and smiles a knowing smile shaded with just the right amount of sadness based on focus group testing, and the huddle breaks up now, and the people start to move on, and the box lowers into the ground, and the gravediggers will bring in the backhoe or whatever to cover him over with soil now, and golly, hopefully he'll rest in peace down there, like he's just resting, just taking a little cat nap inside of a fucking box forever, and like there's any peace in being a stiff, rotting corpse with 10 sword holes gouged into you, but it's all part of God's plan, and it all happens for a reason, and you don't go to funerals, so why are you even here, why would you do this to yourself, why are you here, why are you here, why are you here, right? Right?

CHAPTER 48

And you stand a while over the hole in the Earth, the open mouth swallowing the casket. You stand while the others drift away. You stand because you don't know what else to do.

And you look down past the Astroturf draped around the edges like a terrible green rug. You look into the hard angles etched into the dirt. You look at the shine and curve of the box. You look because you're here.

And a hand grasps your hand, wriggles its fingers between yours, and it's Babinaux, and she looks at you, and you look at her, and you're not as alone as you were. And you know that people care about you, and you care about them, and that it's not all bad, even if it's a lot bad.

You stand together.

You look together.

And you don't have to say anything, and she doesn't have to say anything, and it's for the best this way. Because there are no words for these things inside of you, no turns of phrase that can do these feelings justice, no language to capture what it really means when someone was here and now they're gone.

There are no words, but it's OK, because words aren't your only friend anymore.

CHAPTER 49

I walk over the grass in the cemetery, feeling reconnected to myself, at least a little. I walk alone. Babinaux went off on her own at some point. I haven't seen her in a while. The sun comes out from behind clouds and glares off of the shiny bits on the newer, glossier headstones.

Yeah, the sun shines down like it's just another day, and I guess it is. Not for me, but in the general sense it is. Time holds us down and snuffs us out eventually. All of us. One at a time. The sun is indifferent to this notion.

I walk on a dirt path now. It's a straight shot to the gate that leads into the parking lot where Babinaux's car sits. I can see some movement in the lot, people milling around and talking, cars pulling out, people moving on. This party is over, I guess. The lot remains a ways off, though, and there's not a soul between the gate and me. Just a few of those gigantic pine trees and a lot of graves.

So I answer the question I keep asking myself as I walk this path:

I am here because it felt like the right thing to do. Not for other people. For me. I don't know why. At the moment it doesn't seem that it was a worthy course of action in most ways, but I think maybe it will later, maybe a long time from now. Eventually, I will be glad I did this... maybe. Hard to say.

I don't go to funerals. Remember that tirade? Way back before all of this even really got started, it felt like one of my core beliefs. I wasn't interested in forms of reality beyond what I feel, right? I didn't go to funerals. I didn't go to hospitals. I didn't go out to eat.

Well, here I am. I did it. So have I changed? Am I not who I thought I was?

I spit on the ground.

The soles of my shoes grind rocks into the dirt with each step. My feet are sore, tired, as are my eyes. Really, I suppose all of me is pretty worn out. Every muscle aches, every joint creaks, but I shuffle forward anyway, like a zombie pursuing brains.

Are Farber's men looking for me now? Did they know I would go to this funeral? Did they have the decency to let me do that before they continued their pursuit?

I don't know any of these things. Just thinking of Farber gets my jaw clenched, though. The skin between my eyebrows wrinkles. Blood throbs in the veins in my temples. Murder swells in my heart. I feel like smoke should come out when I exhale.

It doesn't.

In fact, my throat seems to close a little as I imagine the smoke. I cough once, and my chest constricts and seizes up. It won't expand no matter how many times I will it to. I bang a fist into my ribcage to try to jar something loose. When that fails, I bring my hands to the place where the neck and collar bone meet, fingers scraping and scrabbling at my flesh like I might be able to wrench something loose and fix it.

What is this?

Red on the Inside

I try to yell for help, but my mouth only emits wet sounds, guttural sounds like a cat purring underwater. I see my reflection in the glossy black gravestone next to me, my face gone red, bloated, strained.

I collapse there, writhing in the dirt flecked with bits of gravel, 15 feet shy of the gate where people just on the other side talk and laugh and enjoy the company of friends and relatives.

CHAPTER 50

When I wake, the odd bloat still surges in my face, that unnatural warmth and overfilled feeling, but I can breathe. I take in a deep lungful of air to celebrate this fact, finding it a touch on the humid side, almost like breathing in a mist. Too lazy to open my eyes just yet, I swing an arm out next to me to feel at my surroundings. My arm finds no resistance, though. It flails at empty space and returns to where it was – dangling beyond my head.

Oh.

Great.

I open my eyes, and I'm not surprised. I probably should be surprised, but I am not.

I find myself in the alley again – my alley - hanging upside down. It all looks to be in order – the water filled pothole I've fallen in many a time, the dumpster housing the dead dog, I even see the downspout I once climbed down at the far end. Those were good times, yeah? Little has changed. Perhaps the gray seems a touch grayer than I remembered, but it's close enough. It's all the same to me.

And that question echoes in my head one more time for good measure. I suppose it applies in so many ways now:

"Why are you here?"

AWAKE IN THE DARK

Want to read what happens to Grobnagger next? *Back in Black* (Awake in the Dark Book 4) is available on Amazon.

SPREAD THE WORD

Thank you for reading! We'd be very grateful if you could take a few minutes to review it on Amazon.

How grateful? Eternally. Even when we are old and dead and have turned into ghosts, we will be thinking fondly of you and your kind words. The most powerful way to bring our books to the attention of other people is through the honest reviews from readers like you.

COME PARTY WITH US

We're loners. Rebels. But much to our surprise, the most kickass part of writing has been connecting with our readers. From time to time, we send out newsletters with giveaways, special offers, and juicy details on new releases.

Sign up for our mailing list at:
http://ltvargus.com/mailing-list/

ABOUT THE AUTHORS

Tim McBain writes because life is short, and he wants to make something awesome before he dies. Additionally, he likes to move it, move it.

You can connect with Tim on Twitter at @realtimmcbain or via email at tim@timmcbain.com.

L.T. Vargus grew up in Hell, Michigan, which is a lot smaller, quieter, and less fiery than one might imagine. When not click-clacking away at the keyboard, she can be found sewing, fantasizing about food, and rotting her brain in front of the TV.

If you want to wax poetic about pizza or cats, you can contact L.T. (the L is for Lex) at ltvargus9@gmail.com or on Twitter @ltvargus.

TimMcBain.com
LTVargus.com

Made in the USA
Las Vegas, NV
10 November 2023

80605855R00150